T0193944

THE CISTERN

James N. Ezell

authorHOUSE®

AuthorHouse™
1663 Liberty Drive
Bloomington, IN 47403
www.authorhouse.com
Phone: 1 (800) 839-8640

Published by AuthorHouse 11/03/2017

ISBN: 978-1-5462-1441-0 (sc)
ISBN: 978-1-5462-1440-3 (e)

Library of Congress Control Number: 2017916387

Print information available on the last page.

To all who love a good story.

With special thanks to Carol, Jon, Laura, Mae,
Ruth, Pat, Guy,
Members of the Tuscaloosa Writers and Illustrators Guild,
And the Staff of the Hoole Special Collections Library
At the University of Alabama

PROLOGUE

STRONG HANDS WEARING latex gloves forced the bound and gagged man to his knees. His weave swept forward and a tiny Derringer pistol with a single twenty-two caliber round in its upper chamber pressed against the back of his head just above the juncture of his spine and skull. The Derringer popped and the man pitched forward. The bullet had exploded his brain stem. He did not thrash or twitch, his life simply ceased. A trickle of blood oozed from the tiny entrance wound but it was quickly with a large adhesive bandage. Anyone walking by the warehouse would have heard only a faint thump—a car trunk closing, perhaps a door slamming—just another unremarkable urban sound.

Without comment, the men emptied the corpse's pockets and zipped him into a body bag that was loaded into the back of an older model pickup. Several pieces of plastic lawn furniture were tied down over and around him. A rollup door activated and the truck exited the warehouse. It turned onto U. S. Highway 78 West and left the English Avenue Neighborhood of Atlanta. Traffic was light since most commuters had already reached the western suburbs. There would be towns such as Austell, Douglasville, and

Villa Rica before they crossed into Alabama. The radio's clock read a quarter to eight. *Central time now,* thought the driver, but he did not bother to reset it.

The pickup blended unnoticed with the traffic. The driver legitimately owned the vehicle. He meticulously kept up his auto insurance and the glove compartment contained a valid tag receipt and registration. Both men carried disposable cellphones and neither possessed a weapon. The cab's overhead interior light had a burned out bulb—thus no one could see inside at night when a door opened. Drugs or drug use were never allowed in or even near the truck. A drug sniffing dog would be unimpressed and probable cause for a search avoided. In case of an emergency or breakdown both carried ample cash.

By now the little Derringer had been reduced to an amorphous lump of metal by an acetylene torch and tossed into a bin of scrap for recycling. The man's cellphone, jewelry, keys, and wallet suffered a similar fate.

"What's gonna happen with our load?" asked the passenger.

"We're dropping the lawn furniture off at my aunt's place."

"Man, ya know what I mean—the guy in that bag."

"Don't know. And don't wanna know."

"Dontcha wonder?"

"Sure, but don't ever ask me or anyone else again. If they ever strapped one of those lie detectors on us, we'd be telling the truth. Furniture for my aunt, that's all we know. Got the receipt right here," he said patting his pocket.

Since crossing the state line, the thin crescent moon ahead of them had sunk below the cloud tops looming above the horizon. Occasionally a quick flash lit the inside of the clouds as if they blanketed a distant battlefield. An approaching weather front was bringing thundershowers and rain for a couple of days. *Good*, thought the driver, *just go with the flow—fewer cops working traffic.*

At Oxford they turned south on Alabama Highway 21 past fast food joints, cheap motels, and payday loan shops. *Legalized loan sharking—chump change. That ain't shit compared to our take.*

They continued on through Talladega and Sylacauga and then headed southwestward along county roads. Their destination was a little over three hours away.

Thunder rumbled and lightning flashed, followed by constant light rain. They drove in silence passing small towns and nameless rural communities—finally reaching Whitby. The streetlights reflected off the wet pavement of nearly empty streets and the truck's tires bumped across a series of potholes. *Left on 95*, thought the driver.

In minutes the town passed and they were back in darkness. The wipers gently thumped and occasionally squeaked. They turned left on an entrance road, paused in front of a metal gate, and turned off the headlights. "The key's in a hole on the backside of the post down low. Be careful there's a fire ant bed at the bottom." The gate squeaked as it swung open.

Gravel covered the single lane drive across the pasture but in the darkness the truck's left side tires slid off the edge into the slick, sticky mud.

"Damn it!" whispered the driver as he jerked back onto the gravel and stopped. "This spot'll hafta do."

"Ain't we supposed to put him over in that tall grass?"

"That mud's too sticky! I don't wanna track it in the truck. Besides it's half a mile to the road and he'll be gone before daylight. No one'll see him."

They moved the lawn furniture aside. The men grasped the body bag handles and lugged it over to the rutted muddy edge of the drive. The driver cut open one end of the bag and the body slid out onto the gravel. He stuffed a sandwich bag filled with money under the waistband of the corpse's pants, rolled up a brick in the body bag, and wrapped it tightly with duct tape. Later they would throw the bundle from a bridge over a cypress swamp south of Prattville.

After securing the furniture, the truck turned around, exited the property, and went south on Highway 95. The driver always returned by a different route—this time over to Montgomery, where they delivered the lawn furniture to his aunt. They returned to Atlanta by Interstate 85 and arrived in time for morning choir practice.

Back in Tombigbee County the corpse of a young man known as "Six-Bits" lay face up in the rain and remained there until that evening.

1

THE CHEVY TAHOE headed north on a wet, almost deserted highway. Suddenly, as if a switch had been thrown, light exploded across Dalton's peripheral vision. He quickly flipped down the visor and swung it across to cover the driver's side window. Genevieve awoke with a start. The setting sun had broken through the clouds to the west. The roadside came alive with a blanket of red clover, young prairie grasses, and spring wildflowers. To the east a red-tinted rainbow arched across the sky. Dalton pulled off at a pasture turnout and with camera in hand stepped up to a gate. Grass stretched perhaps a quarter mile or more to trees lining a small stream. The field beyond was brightly illuminated.

"Great," whispered Dalton as he stood in awe, "this will look fantastic in my show!" Instinctively he went through a mental checklist—focus carefully, zoom out to wide angle, include some close vegetation on the edge of the frame, think of pools of light and layers of images, bracket the exposures and shoot several frames. The field beyond the trees piqued his interest. He zoomed in and fired off a final shot as the light began to fade and the scene before him dimmed until it was almost totally dark. "That didn't last long," he said turning towards the Tahoe.

"That's a beautiful browse line on those trees," said Genevieve from the car. "It looks like a hedge that's clipped from the bottom and that red rainbow really stood out!" Indeed the cattle had stripped off the leaves and twigs as high as they could reach. And the rainbow had glowed with the same colors as the briefly lit clouds.

They continued north on Alabama Highway 95 across Tombigbee County and the Alabama Black Belt toward Tuscaloosa. "I love this landscape," said Genevieve. "It's so different from anywhere else. It was so much fun growing up here. Remember when we hunted fossils on those white chalk riverbanks and your grandfather showed us those tickle-tongue trees and honey locust with four-inch thorns. I loved show and tell in science class at the middle school, especially with you sitting behind me."

As they neared the county line, a momentary break in the low hanging clouds revealed a towering thunderhead towards the east. The sun had almost disappeared below the horizon but enough light remained to illuminate the top of the cloud that stood several miles high. To Dalton it seemed as if a portal had opened revealing the gigantic statue of some ancient pagan king or demi-god bathed in golden light. Genevieve had fallen asleep again so the moment remained private. She would get in a good forty minutes before they reached Tuscaloosa.

After supper Dalton downloaded the photos. The first shots looked better than expected. After some minor cropping and slight color intensification, the wide angle view of the pasture and rainbow was stunning. A few more like this and he would be ready for a one-man show at Tuscaloosa's Dinah Washington Cultural Arts Center.

"What do you think of this one?" He appreciated her eye for aesthetics.

She looked over his shoulder. "That looks fantastic. Maybe you could come up with another usable image by cropping it further to show just the trees along that branch. I like the way their neatly trimmed undersides contrast with their ragged tops and how the field beyond is visible. Look at it while I cut the pecan pie. Just this once, I'll even put a scoop of real ice cream on yours!"

That last photo! I almost forgot it. The optical zoom lens had maintained the camera's high resolution no matter the setting and as he opened the file the image popped into sharp focus.

Nice three dimensional effects and beautiful layering plus the field road bisects the whole scene drawing viewers into the image. Something looked odd. He blew the image up to better examine an area beyond the trees. He leaned closer and squinted at the screen. Maybe it was an illusion, maybe it was just mud beside the rutted road, but beyond the browse line, on the edge of a shadow, and prone on the edge of the gravel drive, was what appeared to be the foreshortened profile of a human head.

"Genn, take a look at this," he said softly as she returned with their dessert. "Do you see what I see?"

"What is it?" She pushed her glasses higher on her nose and tilted her head back so she could see better from the bottom of her glasses. *I hate wearing glasses ... I'm just too young for bifocals.* "Well, show me what you're talkin' about."

He tapped the screen. "Right here, do you see it?"

"Not really, let me sit down. Slide your laptop over so I can get a good look. What is it you see?" There appeared to be only light and shadow, nothing caught her attention.

He took a slender pen and gently outlined the profile. "Look carefully, isn't that a human face looking toward the sky? It's as if a body's hidden in the shadows and only its head is lit by the sunlight. The features are kinda scrunched up because of the angle of view, see the chin and nose?"

"That's just gumbo mud pushed up where someone ran off the edge of the gravel. It's not a body. Eat your dessert before the ice cream melts."

"Maybe it's my 'magination," he mumbled with a full mouth. The warm pie and vanilla ice cream were deliciously rich.

It had been a long drive home after visiting relatives. They retired early and within minutes fell asleep. When Dalton awoke it was a few minutes past two. Except for Genn's soft breathing the house seemed quieter than usual. His mind raced, the image on the laptop nagging him. *Was that actually a face?*

Even as a child he sometimes interpreted images as different from reality. Once in the third grade he thought an unusual golden-haired animal with a long tail was clinging to a tree trunk outside the classroom window. He had excitedly pointed it out to his teacher. The other children laughed when Miss Ina reminded him and the class that a few days before a large limb had fallen from the tree and that freshly torn bark and splintered wood had created an illusion. Another time while visiting the graves of his parents, a large splotch of mildew or mold on the backside of an old marble tombstone looked like the silhouette of

4

someone in a long robe. He closed his eyes. He would not let his mind play tricks on him again. But no sooner was he asleep than a figure with glowing red eyes appeared at the foot of his bed. *Who are you?*

You know who I am, the figure whispered.

Dalton frequently endured nightmares after the loss of his mother and father. The robed figure often appeared—never threatening but always standing near.

Quietly Dalton arose from bed, slipped on jogging pants, and padded towards the dining room. Sitting in the dark, he again studied the image of the face beyond the browse line and zoomed even closer. Viewed at extreme magnification a single pixel seemed to indicate a nostril. "What's in that shadow?" he whispered as he flattened the contrast.

"Chatting with Jake from State Farm?" Genn said yawning from the doorway.

"Hon, I couldn't sleep. This image keeps bugging me and I thought that with a little manipulation I'd see what's in the shadow."

"Put that away and come back to bed. It's already early Sunday morning and we're going to church in a few hours."

Dalton finally dozed off and awoke when the automatic coffee pot beeped at a quarter past seven. Slightly groggy he went to the kitchen. Genn was already pouring two cups. "Any pie left?" Dalton asked hopefully with a yawn.

"It's in the freezer. Have a bowl of bran with fat free milk and a banana instead—better for you!"

Dalton's lip curled as he mumbled something about recycled cardboard. "Think I'll take the coffee and banana but with a couple pieces of Melba toast instead."

"That's good. By the way, why not contact Sherwyn over at the Special Collections Library tomorrow? He might know something about that place in the photo. Remember, he's done a lot of historical research down there."

2

DALTON RANDOLPH AND Genevieve Hastings were born in Tombigbee County, or as many locals called it "Big Tom." They went to different elementary schools and first met at the middle school in Whitby, the county seat.

Quiet and modest, Genevieve learned to swim and play sports at an early age. In middle school she participated in track and cross country. Her parents' cattle and catfish farm and their neighbor's adjacent property provided a safe and challenging venue for running. She often arose at dawn or earlier to run as much as ten miles across the pastures and through the woods covering the rolling countryside. After school she ran with her team at the local golf course and sometimes invited them to run at her family's place.

Her coach insisted on good nutrition for all her athletes. Consequently she developed a slender fit physique and an interest in dietetics that eventually led to her academic career as a college professor. Her athletic training instilled her with tenacity and the belief that women should be assertive, fit, and independent. As an adult she ran frequently and occasionally rock climbed at the University Recreation Center.

Dalton lost his parents in an auto accident when he was in elementary school. His grandparents became his guardians. Many autumn and winter days he and his grandfather hunted the open countryside or dark bottomland forests near the river. In spring and summer he found fishing to be a quiet pastime that taught patience and perseverance.

Genevieve had hated her name, curly red hair, freckles, slender build, and glasses. Sometimes classmates shouted or whispered, "Genny-Veeee, Genny-Veeee," while some of the meaner ones sang the old song about the skinny girl, "Bony Maronie."

Edgar Wellton, the school bully, sometimes yelled in an exaggerated accent, "Ya look stupid, foe-eyes" or even "Hey red, ya har's on far!"

She hoped it would end once they reached middle school, but Edgar continued his aggression. On the first day of seventh grade classes Edgar shoved her against the metal lockers lining the hallway. She winced in pain as her arm and head struck the hasps and padlocks.

Dalton was close behind. Grabbing Edgar he hissed between clinched teeth. "Why'd you do that?"

Edgar sneered contemptuously, "Because she's ugly!"

Dalton slammed him into the concrete block wall and struck him in the face as hard as he could. The bully stared in disbelief as he grabbed his mouth and blood ran between his fingers.

"What's this? What's this?" shouted Mr. Simon as he stepped from the doorway of his classroom. "What happened?"

"He was running down the hall and knocked me into

the lockers and then ran into the wall," said Genevieve with a slightly pained, yet impish, smile.

"Yeah Mr. Simon, that's what happened. I saw it!" chimed in Sherwyn Scott standing nearby.

"That's what I saw too," added Billie Schroader coming around the corner.

Mr. Simon grabbed Edgar's arm and led him away.

"Thanks for standing up to him. He's such a jerk face!" said Genevieve as Dalton and Sherwyn helped pick up her glasses, books, and crushed lunch bag. There was liquid oozing across the paper. Earlier in the summer, fire had damaged the school lunch room and students brown-bagged for a couple of months until repairs were complete.

"What do those initials, 'SWS', on your shirt stand for?" asked Genn.

Sherwyn laughed and shook his head. "Mom had this monogrammed, the letters stand for 'Sherwyn Williams Scott,' and yeah—you guessed it—my parents run the paint store here in Whitby. I'm what some of the other kids call a 'townie.'"

"Hey Sherwyn, I'm Genn Hastings and this is Billie June Schroader. We went to the elementary school down at Coleman's Corner. And you," she said smiling at Dalton, "what's your name?"

"Da-Da-Dalton," he stammered. "Dalton Randolph, we live over near the river. I went to the Gum Pond School."

Genn nudged him with her elbow. "Oh yeah, we called your little football team the 'Gummy Bears.'"

"Were you a cheerleader?" asked Dalton.

"Me—a cheerleader? No way! If mom woulda let me I'd

have been on the field playing ball and none of y'all coulda caught me!"

"I've heard they're gonna close those schools next year and bus the kids up here," said Sherwyn.

"I hate that," said Billie. "It took nearly an hour on the bus this morning, that's way too long for the little ones, especially my twin brothers and Genn's sister, Lillian. They'll be bouncing off the ceiling!"

"What about that kid Mr. Simon hauled to the principal's office?" asked Sherwyn.

"That's Edgar," said Genn. "He went to our elementary school. He's always been a bully and troublemaker. And for some reason he picks on me all the time. Dalton, you're the first person who's ever hit him back. Lillian kicked him once but it didn't seem to do any good."

"I don't think he'll be causing any more trouble—at least not for us," said Sherwyn.

The lunch bell sounded. "Let's go eat," said Dalton.

"Yeah," chimed in Sherwyn standing nearby, "it looks like Edgar ruined your lunch. Mom packed too much and Dalton needs to diet a little."

"And I have an extra Twinkie," interjected Billie, "so there'll be plenty for the four of us. And by the way, I'm dropping the name June. Please, just call me Billie from now on."

As they walked toward lunch, Dalton lightly touched Genevieve's arm. "Does that hurt? Looks like there's gonna be a bruise."

"It's not a problem, just another 'freckle', but a little bigger," she said wiping her glasses.

How could that creep say she's ugly? thought Dalton. He

enjoyed listening to an "oldies" radio station that played sixties and seventies music—the songs of his parents' youth. *She's the girl Sugarloaf sang about—the 'Green-Eyed Lady!'* He smiled as the sound of the song's lengthy Hammond B-3 organ solo throbbed in his head and lightened his step.

One of Dalton's fondest high school memories happened in August before their senior year when they were seventeen. Tombigbee County sweltered and in the distance, ripples of heat rose and mirages that looked like pools of liquid mercury snaked across the highways. Genn and Dalton had driven to the backside of his grandparents' place almost three miles from the front gate. The headwaters of a tributary of Chulahomma Creek began near the far property line. A seasonal drainage way ran through a copse of hackberry and cedar trees. On one side stood a single Osage orange, known in the local vernacular as a "bodock" tree—its branches loaded with huge lime-green fruit that looked like alien brains. In the shady center lay a large oval depression cut into the white chalk by centuries of runoff from downpours.

"What a beautiful spot," said Genn. "Do y'all swim here?"

"We don't get back here much now 'cept to check the fences. The cows used to wade out and drink from this pool but we moved 'em to another pasture back in the spring. I've never seen it so clean or the water this clear. Those heavy rains a couple of days ago must've flushed it out."

"Let's give it a try," she said with raised eyebrows.

"But we don't have our swim suits."

"Not needed," she said as she slipped from her

clothes—her alabaster skin speckled by little patches of sunlight filtering through the leaves above.

Dalton stood in wild-eyed wonder as she jumped in the cool water. He couldn't move and tried to look aside.

"Oh this is so nice! Come on in!"

"I don't know," he said haltingly.

"Dalton Randolph! You're blushing. Don't be embarrassed, take off those sweaty clothes and join me."

"Well, I guess no one'll see us back here," he stammered still frozen in place.

"Are you or aren't you coming in?"

"Okay," he said reluctantly as he pulled off his boots and tee shirt, unbuckled his belt, and stepped out of his jeans.

"Polka-dot boxer shorts!" giggled Genn with both hands covering her mouth.

"Granny got 'em for me."

"Your grandmother buys your underwear?" Genn laughed out loud. Dalton could feel his face burning. "Well, take 'em off and come on in."

"If it's all the same to you, I'll keep 'em on. Aren't you being an exhibitionist?"

"Look Dalton, there're no boys around our house except for Dad and he's gone much of the time. My little sister and I never wear much at home. Billie Schroader spends a lot of time at our house and all of us skinny-dip in the pool out back but usually after sundown. Lillian and I have too many freckles already."

"So y'all are nudists?"

"Of course not! We like to be comfortable in warm weather and our folks don't care as long as we're discreet."

"This doesn't seem very discreet," he said as he waded in the cool water.

"Well, it is and besides you're the boy I've fallen in love with. Haven't you ever wondered what I really look like under my track outfit?"

"Yes, but …."

"But what?" she asked as she splashed water in his face. Dalton smiled and reached for her but she pulled away. "Get a good look, but no touching!" she laughed.

Dalton, Genevieve, Sherwyn, and Billie were friends all through their high school years. They frequented events together and occasionally double-dated. Sherwyn was very personable and a friend to all. Extroverted Billie's shenanigans kept her fellow students snickering and her in constant trouble that included a suspension for hoisting a dead alligator up the school flagpole. But Dalton and Genevieve were studious, slightly introverted, and constant comfortable companions. At their senior prom Genevieve wore a stunning green velvet dress that complimented her hair and matched her eyes. When they made their entrance every head turned and the crowd applauded. "They clean up pretty good, don't they?" Sherwyn said nudging Billie.

All four entered the University of Alabama the fall semester of that year. Dalton studied civil engineering with an emphasis on rural water supply while Genevieve majored in dietetics. They married during the spring break of their senior year and after graduation moved to Tallahassee, Florida for graduate school. Sherwyn, once the social gadfly and chronic changer of academic direction, became an archivist and historian. Billie began in the aerospace engineering program but dropped out when her father died. She returned to Tombigbee County to help with the family cattle farm.

Armed with their PhDs, Dalton and Genn applied for positions at numerous colleges and universities. One of Dalton's professors at the University of Alabama retired leaving a vacancy for which there were hundreds of applicants. However, because of an impressive list of publications and additional study of geology and groundwater, Dalton was hired and became an Assistant Professor of Civil Engineering. Genn initially worked as an instructor in the College of Human Environmental Sciences. She received excellent evaluations by her students and co-workers and eventually advanced to also become an assistant professor. Not only were they Dr. and Dr. Randolph, they were now the Professors Randolph.

Dalton and Genn lived in a one-story house in one of the older subdivisions off Rice Valley Road. They bought the house ten years earlier at a bargain price from the estate of an elderly man who had become a recluse and for many years neglected even the most basic maintenance tasks.

It took months of work—new roof and HVAC system, refinished floors, tree removal, etc.—but finally they left their apartment near campus and moved in. *Welcome to suburbia and a mortgage*, thought Dalton as he reminisced about the trials, tribulations, and joys of working with Genn to do most of the work themselves.

Because of her slender athletic build, Genn was adept at scrambling into narrow reaches of the attic and crawl space—places Dalton couldn't reach. Genn seemed happiest when she donned a face mask and rubber gloves for the grubbiest tasks. She always smiled and said "I do the dirty work in the tight spots and save us big bucks."

Although there were occasional arguments, harsh words, and hurt feelings, they persevered through months of late night and weekend work and finally their efforts bore fruit—a completely remodeled home with a value far exceeding its purchase price and cost of renovation.

"Darling, I love you," he said as they moved in on their tenth anniversary.

"Dalton, things are going so well, let's give more thought to adopting—maybe in the next couple of years."

"Well, we did all these renovations with all the adoption safety concerns in mind. There shouldn't be any major problems with the house. Nice airy rooms with lotsa light, plus we've met all the building codes, especially fire safety and access requirements. Let's start the process by collecting info on furniture for a nursery. But also let's see what's needed for older children. Infants can be difficult to find."

Adoption had been on their minds for several years since their efforts to have a child had proved futile. Conception just didn't occur and the expense of embryo transplantation far exceeded their means. They finally came to the conclusion that starting a family the traditional way was unlikely. Besides, Genn especially liked the idea of providing a loving home to a child who didn't have one.

"What do you think you'd like?" she asked.

"Happy and healthy are the most important things— boy or girl doesn't matter. Of course red hair and green eyes aren't required, but they would be bonuses."

Genn smiled and shook her head. She loved Dalton's obsession with her hair and eyes. "But hopefully without so much curl and glasses."

3

"KNOW ANYTHING ABOUT this area back home? I took some photos from the road and something strange shows up in one of them." Dalton said to voice mail and then added GPS coordinates.

Uncharacteristically Sherwyn Scott checked his voice mail a few minutes later as he returned from a yawn-inspiring staff meeting. He typed in the coordinates.

Interesting, he thought as Google Earth flew to the location. *That's on Alabama 95 south of Whitby.*

He zoomed closer until the image converted to street level view. *I cannot imagine how many miles are put on those Google cars.* He rotated the street view until it faced east. A mail box sat upon a post and beside it a metal gate stood across the entrance to the property. *I know this place—Saint-Cyr! Too bad that Google car couldn't go down that entrance drive.*

He exited the street level view and moved east across the property. The image date was recent, only a few months earlier back in the winter. A herd of cattle stood scattered across the field, their bodies casting short shadows. A small stream flowed north/south across the property. Narrow strips of trees lined the banks on either side. Beyond the stream he could see a few scattered trees—some probably bodock, others cedar. Further to the east sat a small mobile home or possibly construction site trailer. A blue pickup sat beside it along with what appeared to be rusting farm equipment.

He returned Dalton's call. "Hey, that's the old Faustin place—Saint-Cyr. Looks like someone lives on the backside in an old trailer, it's probably not visible from the highway because of the trees."

"I don't think I've ever heard that name before, at least not back in Big Tom. Is it Cajun or something?"

"It's French, not Cajun. Henri Faustin served as a young lieutenant in Napoleon's army in the last couple of years of the Spanish Peninsular War. He named his place after a distant cousin, Marshall Saint-Cyr who got him his commission."

"How did someone like that wind up in Tombigbee County?"

"That's quite a story. Got a few minutes?"

"Sure, my next class isn't for an hour," said Dalton with a smile and eye roll since Sherwyn loved long tales. *No way this'll be a 'few minutes.'*

"Well, after Napoleon's abdication in 1815, Faustin was accused of committing atrocities against the families of Spanish guerilla fighters. He fled to New Orleans, but word of his crimes reached some of Louisiana's Spanish population. France nominally controlled Louisiana before the 1803 purchase but New Orleans was primarily a Spanish City. Those times are not well documented but there are letters and diaries that tell of assassination attempts and duels. I've always laughed when someone refers to the 'French Quarter.' In truth the historic buildings are Spanish."

"So he left and came to Alabama?"

"Yeah, a couple of years later, about the time Congress created the Alabama Territory. You might say he went into hiding by fleeing into the wilderness. He acquired a large tract of Black Belt Prairie land and set up a plantation. About that time a number of towns were founded but he stayed on the place. That was unusual back then since most planters lived in small towns on the periphery. Remember the old sayin' about Black Belt gumbo mud, 'in summer ya leave no footprints, but in winter ya take 'em with ya.'"

"Do I ever!" exclaimed Dalton. "Genn and I got stuck one time on my grandfather's place after a thunderstorm and had to walk out a couple of miles. After every step we got half an inch taller and every few yards we had to sling that crap off the bottoms of our boots. That didn't bother Genn, but my knees ached for a week."

"That mud made overland travel almost impossible in winter so most planters didn't build their main residences out there. That's why you see those big old places in towns like Whitby, Greensboro, or Eutaw. Faustin lived out there, but probably because he wanted to remain isolated. He even avoided the nearby exiles from France and the slave revolt in Haiti who settled the French lands set aside by Congress over near Demopolis."

"Did he have a lot of slaves?"

"Yeah, hundreds, and he drove the field hands mercilessly. Even though the Atlantic slave trade was outlawed by then, he paid smugglers to bring in more since so many died. I think he also wanted slaves directly from Africa that didn't speak English so if they ran away they couldn't tell how they'd been treated or where they came from. Slaves built the big mansion, but they didn't belong to Faustin. They were trained builders he hired from someone in Tuscaloosa."

"It all sounds horrible," said Dalton.

"When my grandfather was young, back in the forties, he knew some of the descendants of Faustin's house servants. They told him the slaves who worked in the mansion were treated better than the field hands and that he kept one of them, a beautiful young quadroon named Marie, as his mistress. Those were awful times and he was considered to be particularly brutal as he would have slaves lashed for even the most trivial things. He eventually made a fortune in cotton. Then almost went broke in the financial collapse of 1837. It's said he was addicted to laudanum, a solution of raw opium in alcohol, and drank himself to near insanity with absinthe. In the 1840s he whipped a slave to death and believe it or not was sentenced to sixteen years in prison. He disappeared before serving a day and was never seen again. Afterwards there were rumors of voodoo and the devil gettin' his due. But in reality the slaves practiced voodoo as a way to maintain some of their African traditions and protect themselves from the brutality of their masters. Of course the tale of the Devil came from his name which translates as 'Faust,' the man who sold his soul in German legends and Goethe's novel.

"What happened to the slaves and Faustin's family?"

"Most of the slaves ran away but were likely arrested. Some were returned but since many didn't speak English and didn't know where they came from, they were resold. Faustin's wife supposedly died of despair a couple of years later. His son took over and stabilized the finances but never regained the wealth old Henri wasted. It passed to a grandson who changed his name. That's why growing up we never knew any Faustins."

"What about the place? Is anything out there?"

"The property remained in his family over much of the next century and then the mansion burned in the early forties. At the time local newspapers reported that the smoke could be seen from four surrounding counties. You know how heart pine burns—a lotta heat and black smoke. Those same newspapers later reported that a rich banker from Birmingham bought the place at a tax auction and raised cattle on it for several years. Of course I always heard he used it as a retreat for his gambling and drinking buddies— some place they could get away to on weekends to party with their girlfriends. There used to be a joke that their wives stayed home in Mountain Brook because their high heels would bog down in the mud."

"It must've been something to see."

"I heard the banker salvaged lumber from some of the slave cottages to build a camp house but it probably rotted down years ago. But you can see what the big house looked like. The HABS work done during the Depression documented it with lots of photos and drawings. Go to the Library of Congress website … it's all there online. I doubt much survives on the site except a few bricks, lots of broken glass from liquor bottles, and some bulb plants like irises and daffodils. Oh, and by the way, be careful about repeating that story back home, there are people of both races descended from him and his slaves. As far as I know nobody kept the surname."

"That's quite a story! Who owns the place now?"

"There's a tale that the banker lost the place in a card

game, but I don't know who has it now. Check with the tax assessor's office in Whitby. They have an online data base. But what's this *something strange* you saw?"

"I'm not really sure. Genn thinks it's just rutted mud, but it looks like a dead body to me."

"Send it and let me take a look."

"Hang on a minute. There, it's on the way."

"Okay ... just what am I supposed to be seeing?"

"Look beyond the stream crossing and then on the left edge of the road ... see the face, it's like a body's lying face up with its head just outta the shadow."

"I see what you mean, but with the late afternoon light it looks the same as that wet mud. Course the corpse of a white or light-complexioned black person would be about that same color in those lighting conditions," said Sherwyn. "If you're convinced it's a body the law needs to know. Get in touch with Lucius."

"Hey thanks for the information, it feels like I just finished one of your history classes."

"Come by the office tomorrow for the final exam. Buy our lunch and you can CLEP out with an A-plus."

"Yeah, right!" said Dalton with a laugh as he hung up.

Dalton pushed back in his chair after sending a brief message with an enlarged detail cropped from the photo to Deputy Lucius Jones at the Tombigbee County's Sheriff's office. "Whew," he whispered, "I hope he can clear this up."

Dalton finished his only afternoon lecture and returned home. He cooked a light dinner of pan sautéed tuna, baked potato, and salad. "You're learning," said Genn with a smile, "that's a good healthy meal, *if* you lay off the butter, sour cream, and bleu cheese dressing—and that being said, that left-over pecan pie stays in the freezer! But don't look sad, you can have something else for dessert later."

Dalton and Genn loved vintage movies and had recently been introduced to those directed by Alfred Hitchcock. Enthralled they watched *Vertigo*, the story of Scotty Ferguson's obsession with Madeleine Elster—Jimmy Stewart and Kim Novak—set against the backdrop of 1958 San Francisco.

"That movie gave me the chills," said Genn.

"Tomorrow comes early, let's call it a night."

He watched as Genn shed her clothes silhouetted against sheer drapes illuminated only by moonlight. She slipped beneath the covers and their arms encircled each other. The lovers knew each other's body very well.

"Oh, Genn, you're my obsession, I love you so."

4

FRIDAY AFTERNOON, MAY 19, 1989
BUTTERBEAN HOLLOW, TOMBIGBEE COUNTY

A CAR DOOR slammed and heavy footsteps tromped across the rickety porch. A disheveled man stumbled through the front door. "Joel, you're home early," said his wife. "Sumthin wrong?"

"Damn son-of-a-bitch fired me! Claimed I been drankin' and run his tractor off in one of them damned fish ponds."

"Oh Joel, that's so unfair! It musta been an accident."

"Damn right it was! My family useta be the big dogs in this county. Nobody useta treat us like that. We had all kinda land. But it got stolen."

"I never heard of that,"

"No use talkin' 'bout it, nuthin'll ever change. Kin keeps quiet 'bout it.

"When did that happen?"

"Long, long time ago. Foe my grandpa was born. Family's been pore ever since."

"What about the pay he owes you?"

23

"Said fixin' that tractor's more than my pay, so the bastard's keepin' it."

"Oh, Joel, we need that money. There ain't any food in the house."

"Yeah, but there's always booze and cigarettes," said their son Edgar.

Anger flashed wildly in Joel's eyes. "What did you say?"

"You heard me," said Edgar. "Mama and me're hungry. We ain't had nuthin to eat since yesterday!"

Joel unbuckled and pulled off his belt and doubled it up in his hand. Edgar's eyes widened and he tried to flee through the back door but slipped and fell. Joel began savagely beating him.

"No Daddy don't, please, don't!" screamed Edgar as he rolled into a ball on the floor. But his father kept striking him with the wide leather belt.

"Please leave him alone," pleaded Edgar's mother. "Don't hit him anymore—that's enough! He's just a child!"

"Little son-of-a-bitch smarted off again," growled the staggering man.

"He didn't mean it, Joel. Please leave him alone, he's hungry and he's only nine years old."

"Shut up bitch!" he screamed as he punched at his wife, striking a glancing blow to her head. Edgar jumped to his feet and leaped out the back door, running as fast as he could.

Rachel Wellton fell to the floor sobbing. "Please Joel, please calm down, one of these days you gonna kill us."

He stumbled across the room and fell heavily on a tattered, stained sofa. "If that ever happens, it'll be your fault."

Joel and Rachel Wellton lived in a dilapidated house nestled between ridges in a hilly area on the eastern side of

Tombigbee County. There were only a few scattered houses and mobile homes nearby. Overgrown shrubs and chest high weeds obscured the front porch. A dented twenty-year-old car sat in a driveway littered with oil and beer cans and bags of garbage torn open by stray dogs.

Joel passed out from drinking almost every night and frequently became violent before losing consciousness. In earlier years the abuse was verbal but escalated as their only child, Edgar, grew from infancy to the first years of elementary school. Joel often struck his son with a belt or slapped him across the face. Any intervention by Rachel was met with fists and feet.

Joel worked infrequently and what little pay he received went for alcohol and cigarettes. Rachel toiled at minimum wage for long hours at a convenience store—barely keeping the family fed. Many weekends Edgar stayed with his disabled grandmother who hobbled on a cane and seldom uttered anything other than obscenities.

Without parental support Edgar often missed school and lagged far behind his classmates. Without siblings or neighborhood friends his only male role model was his father. In school his behavior reflected that of his abuser—a short temper and bullying of the younger students—especially girls. Often he directed his anger at a skinny red-haired classmate—Genevieve Hastings. To him she was the teacher's pet and a "goody-goody." Edgar never turned in homework, while she was always prepared. Edgar wore tattered, dirty clothes while she was neat and well-groomed. Edgar's teeth were yellow and beginning to decay, but the hated redhead had white teeth and a ready smile. At every opportunity he pushed or hit her and sometimes even snatched her school work and tore it to pieces.

That night Joel lay in a stupor on a sofa that reeked of tobacco smoke, urine, and mildew while Rachel lay sobbing on their bed. Edgar crept back in the house and deftly extracted an old thirty-eight revolver from the drawer of a bedside table. Clutching the rusty weapon with both hands he pressed the barrel against his father's chest. Although the ammunition was decades old, the weapon discharged knocking Edgar backwards onto the floor. The bullet tore through Joel's sternum and shattered the muscle of his heart. He never regained consciousness and died within minutes. There would be no more hunger or beatings.

"Well Deputy, what do *you* think happened here?" asked Sheriff Herbert Mosby as they surveyed the scene.

"Looks like that woman or even her kid shot Wellton while he laid on that couch."

"Naw, that ain't what happened, it's a clear case of suicide—no doubt about it. See how that revolver just rolled outta his hand on to the floor. Give the situation some more thought, look at that poor bruised woman and her son and this dump they live in—plain as day to me!"

The deputy stared at his boss and then glanced around. "Yes sir," he slowly replied.

"Good, glad you concur. Now you need some experience if you're gonna be an investigator one of these days. Look around and take some good notes and photos. Then go back to the office and write up a report just like they taught you in that criminal justice course the county paid for. Meanwhile I'll call the DA and give him a preliminary report. The coroner's people will take care of the body. That woman and her child have suffered enough. I'm takin' 'em to my sister's house. She and some ladies from the church will take care of 'em for a few days."

A week later, Joel Wellton received a simple graveside service in a vacant part of the Coleman's Corner United Methodist Church Cemetery. Rachel had no money for funeral expenses. However, several church members came to her assistance.

Edgar and his mother stared into the open grave. It wasn't the traditional six feet deep. After digging four feet into the dark soil of the Alabama Black Belt, the funeral home's little backhoe could only scratch a few inches more into the gleaming white chalk. After a few words from the minister and a brief prayer the plain coffin sank below the rim of the grave and sat at the bottom. As they walked away, the black man operating the backhoe began filling the hole.

Most of the other residents of the cemetery lay under the shade of ancient cedars. For over a century and a half Homecoming had been a tradition at the church. Each year people visited their deceased loved ones and distant ancestors. They cleaned the monuments and graves and left trinkets or colorful displays of artificial flowers. The air filled with children's laughter, affectionate stories, and the complicated details of family histories since one way or another almost everyone was related. In a far corner Joel Wellton's sunken grave sat in the hot sun unvisited and forgotten—its only marker the conical mound of a large fire ant bed.

5

THE PHONE RANG. "Hey my man, it's Lucius down in Whitby. Hope I didn't interrupt dinner."

"Not at all, I just finished putting the plates in the dishwasher."

"How are you and Genn doin'? Hope y'all are havin' a good semester."

After some chit-chat about their recent high school reunion, Dalton asked, "Well, whadda you think about that photo?"

Lucius paused for a moment. "My afternoon patrol goes by there. I stopped at that gate where you took the photo and got a good look with a spotter scope we use at the firin' range. That thing's good for about sixty times magnification. There just didn't seem to be anything out there."

"Did you go out to the spot?"

"Well, I'd need probable cause or a warrant for that and since nothing was evident, the judge would be reluctant to issue one. You know how it is, all property in Alabama is posted by law and without probable cause, a search warrant, or permission from the property owner, going out there would be trespassing. Since there's a fence, a gate with a stout lock and chain, and posted signs, a person could get thirty days in the boss's hoosegow."

"Lucius, do you know the property owner? I went to the online tax assessor's database and it lists an 'E. Wellton.' Is that Edgar?"

"One and the same. You remember what happened. Several years ago he killed a man in a bar fight just over the state line in Lauderdale County, Mississippi. They tried him for murder but the jury finally convicted him of manslaughter. You might not know this but when he was in prison his uncle Burl Hickam died and left that place to his sister, Edgar's mother. She died a few months later and it passed to Edgar. Hickam was a bootlegger and gambler. Some say he won that place in a poker game back in the fifties. Edgar lives on the backside of the property in his uncle's old camp trailer. Keeps to himself and seems to stay outta trouble, at least on my patch anyway. He got out early a couple of years ago and they allowed him to move back to Alabama since he had that place to live on. We do 'courtesy supervision' since he was doin' time in an outta state prison, but he still has to report to his parole officer in Mississippi. Once in a while they call over here checking on him. He works weekdays as a diesel mechanic's helper over near Meridian."

"Very interesting but I still wonder about what's in that photo."

"Well, we can't do anything else unless there's more to go on. Wish I could be more help."

"Did you notice anything else out there, different or out of the ordinary?" asked Dalton.

"Not out at the property, but a while back I was doin'

some routine checks on him for the Mississippi folks and looked at some records at the Tax Collector's office. One of the clerks told me he pays his property tax in cash—small bills—tens and twenties. You know how low our taxes are, maybe two dollars an acre for land like that. But he's got over twelve hundred acres. That job can't pay much plus he's docked for restitution to the family of the man he killed."

Later that evening Dalton searched the Library of Congress website for the Historical American Buildings Survey for Tombigbee County and found the Faustin Place. The notes described it as a raised French Creole mansion similar to those found in Haiti and places closer such as Mobile or New Orleans. In 1934 a government photographer named Alex Bush made dozens of photos and a draftsman made detailed drawings of the exterior elevations and the interiors along with site and floor plans. The drawings also documented several out-buildings including the kitchen, servants' quarters, and a cistern covered with a small latticed gazebo. Dalton often mentioned in his water supply engineering classes the importance of cisterns in many areas of the world such as North Africa, the Middle East, and India. They were even used in the Black Belt Prairie where there were no springs or groundwater and streams often dried up in summer. Typically a house's gutters drained into a cistern that could hold many thousands of gallons.

Interesting, that may be the only part of the original place still out there.

Lucius and Dalton's friendship started in early childhood. The Jones family property sat adjacent to

Dalton's grandfather's ranch. Lucius' father has been a big football fan—especially of the Dallas Cowboys and their coach Tom Landry. Thus Lucius came by his full name Lucius Landry Jones.

Both entered the Gum Pond Elementary School when they reached six. The little school only had about a hundred students—fewer than twenty per grade. Dalton and Lucius excelled at recess. Each pair of grades—first and second, third and fourth, fifth and sixth—had its own playground. The younger children preferred the swings and slide while the older kids liked more structured play such as makeshift baseball and basketball. Dalton always smiled when he recalled the pecan tree that served as first base.

The little school sat in an isolated part of the county on the outside of Chinaman's Bend on the Tombigbee River high above any potential flood. It received its name just after the Civil War when three Chinese railroad workers drowned after their small boat capsized. The men were said to be Christians by their co-workers and Genn's great-great-grandfather insisted they be buried several miles away next to the Hastings Family Plot in the Coleman's Corner Methodist Church Cemetery. For nearly a century on Chinese New Year a small bouquet of daffodils appeared on their graves.

Blindman's Bluff occupied the highest point on Chinaman's Bend, standing at least sixty feet above the water, its white chalk an easily recognizable landmark for generations of Indians, early settlers, and boatmen. Sometimes during the drier months such as September or October when the river flowed slowly and the water cleared somewhat, an eerie shape loomed beneath the surface.

In 1853 the steamboat *Gondolier,* said to be carrying miners returning from the California gold fields, struggled upstream against a strong current. Captain Clete LeMoyne was hugging the inside of the bend seeking slower current but still his ship strained—barely making headway. In spite of the engineer's protests he called for more steam, but *Gondolier's* boiler couldn't contain the increased pressure. A single rivet shot like a bullet across the engine room. In milliseconds other rivets along the seam came loose in sequence like a demonic zipper. With a deafening roar the boiler exploded, hurling debris high in the air instantly killing most on board.

Her superstructure destroyed, the shattered wreck momentarily drifted but the strong current drove her to the outside of the bend where she rammed the steep chalk bank and settled onto her final resting place.

A young Scotsman returning to his mercantile business in Demopolis had been seated on the aft deck far from the boiler. The explosion threw him into the river where he clung to a cabin door and managed to save three others. Slaves belonging to Genn's ancestor, Zachariah Hastings, searched for survivors and found them the next morning on a downstream sandbar. Hailed as a hero, the merchant later wrote a stirring newspaper account of the disaster.

For more than a century and a half stories persisted of piles of gold nuggets, bars, and coins—the treasure of the returning miners—scattered along the bottom of the river and mingled with the wreckage and passengers' bones. Fishermen began telling stories of hauntings along the Bend—the sounds of unexplained explosions, moans and cries, mists that glowed softly, and lonely ephemeral figures searching the water's edge. Thus was born the Legend of the *Gondolier's* Gold.

Often after school in early autumn, Dalton and Lucius would lay atop Blindman's Bluff their eyes searching for the outline of the ill-fated vessel. More than once Dalton daydreamed aloud. "Man, if we could just find that gold ... we'd be rich!"

But the more practical-minded Lucius would reply, "Yeah, but we're way up here and that old boat's way down there with the alligators and snapping turtles."

Elephant Swamp filled the inside of Chinaman's Bend. Several miles across, it seemed another world since there were no nearby bridges and one had to drive nearly twenty miles to get over there. The swampy terrain was covered by towering cypress, dense stands of tupelo gum, and the occasional hummock. In fall and winter flights of ducks and geese soared overhead. In spring and summer an immense rookery of egrets, herons, and wood storks covering many acres could be seen. Plus there were ominous stories of wild hogs, water moccasins, and alligators of legendary size. Elephant Swamp received its name when a huge skull with tusks was found there in the early 1800s. For many decades it gathered dust in a hallway corner of the courthouse at Whitby until Eugene Allen Smith, the State Geologist, declared it to be from a mastodon, an extinct Ice Age cousin of the elephants. He added it might have drowned trying to cross the river thousands of years earlier.

Lucius and Dalton spent long, languid summers roaming the fields, woods, and streams of Big Tom County. They weren't allowed to fish in the catfish ponds, so they often rode horses over to a neighbor's place to fish in a large pond filled with bluegill bream, bass, and catfish. Years before, beavers had set up housekeeping and made short work of the many willows along the shore. Some of the tree trunks had fallen in the water providing safe haven for sunbathing cooters and sliders that plopped into the water at any unusual sound or disturbance.

Dalton's grandmother often prepared lunch bags stuffed with peanut butter sandwiches and cans of Vienna sausages and a soft-pack cooler with icy cans of Dr. Pepper or Buffalo Rock Ginger Ale.

Their tackle consisted of a Zebco 33 spinning reel mounted on an old rod with a broken cork grip and a bamboo pole rigged with hook, line, and red bobber. Sometimes in the still air a dragonfly or "snake doctor" might land on the bobber.

Often they returned home with a stringer of fish large enough for dinner. Lucius fileted the fish and Mrs. Randolph coated them in a buttermilk cornmeal batter and deep fried them in hot peanut oil. French fries, hushpuppies, and coleslaw rounded out the feast.

6

"EL-SHAWN BATEMAN, STREET name 'Six-Bits,' has been reported missing by his grandmother," said Detective Gabe Garland of the Atlanta Police Department. "Kenny, whadda we know about this guy?"

Detective Kenneth Hilbertson, his tie loosened after a long day, leaned back in his chair, hands behind his head. "Mid-level distributor in the English Avenue Neighborhood—supplies street dealers. My informant over there tells me the word's out he's skimmin'—flashin' money and jewelry, playin' the big dog. Cuttin' a little off the top's expected but ol' Six-Bits been gettin' greedy and the higher-ups are pissed off."

Garland entered Bateman's name in the department database. An image of a young light-complexioned African American male popped up. "Here he is—lots of arrests for domestic violence—slaps around his ladies, but they've always refused to cooperate."

"Think he skipped?"

"Could have, but he might have been taken out—wouldn't surprise me."

"I think something's probably happened to him. I'll

call his grandmother and see if we can go over there in the morning."

The English Avenue Neighborhood of Northwest Atlanta had once been a white working-class area. Racial violence and riots occurred in the sixties and by the seventies it had transitioned into an open-air heroin market with rampant prostitution. The detectives drove along narrow streets lined with weedy vacant lots, graffitied dumpsters, and litter. In spite of redevelopment projects and investment by the city it remained a high-crime area with over half its housing units abandoned. After decades of living under near-siege conditions, a few elderly residents still clung to their homes.

Garland rang the doorbell of a somewhat dilapidated craftsman cottage with an overgrown front yard. Burglar bars covered the windows and a formidable looking wrought iron security door protected the entrance. After a moment the inside wooden door opened perhaps an inch.

"Who is it?" Someone with a soft voice asked as a wary eye peered at the detectives and their badges.

"Mrs. Bateman we're with the Atlanta Police Department. I'm Detective Garland and this is Detective Hilbertson. We're here to talk to you about your grandson. May we come in?"

"Yes, please do," she said cautiously as she unlatched three door chains.

They entered a living room furnished with old, but clean serviceable furniture, the air filled with a pleasant aroma.

"Excuse the smell," said Mrs. Bateman. "I'm baking a sweet potato pie for a neighbor who's doin' poorly."

"Umm," said Garland. "That smells wonderful, reminds me of my childhood back in Macon."

"Please have a seat."

"Tell us about your grandson," said Hilbertson.

"I did my best to raise him but he's had a troubled life."

"What about his parents?"

"His mama died of an overdose when he was a baby. His daddy, my son, is dead for all I know. He only came 'round every few weeks, whenever he needed money or a meal. But he stopped showin' up about ten years ago when El-Shawn was eleven or twelve. We don't know if he's dead or in prison somewhere."

"So you raised El-Shawn?" asked Garland.

"I tried, but my husband Zeke got hurt on the railroad and I spent most of my time back then takin' care of him. El-Shawn grew up on the streets like all the kids 'round here. I did the best I could but he kept gettin' in trouble at school—mostly bullying the younger kids and stealing. He spent a lot of time in juvenile detention."

"Does he have a job?"

"No, but he's always got money. Claims he does odd jobs to help his three baby-mommas. But I know he deals like of a lotta folks 'round here."

"When did you last see him?" asked Garland.

"Wednesday ... two weeks ago."

"That would be April thirteenth," said Hilbertson as he took notes. "When were you expecting to see him again?"

"He usually comes 'round every two, three days. Said he was comin' to Sunday dinner but never showed up."

"Is that unusual?"

"Most times he's pretty good 'bout showin' up when he says he's gonna. But he ain't ever been gone this long a time."

"Do you know the names of his girlfriends and where they live?"

"There's Jamayka, Sweet, and some white junky he calls 'Li'l Angel.' That's all I know 'cept they all have his babies."

"Know where any of 'em live?"

"Mostly street corners."

"What about El-Shawn's children?"

"A couple of the littlest ones are in foster care. I don't know 'bout the other three. Maybe they're living with their mommas' families. I'd take care of some of 'em but my heart's bad."

"And your grandson? Where does he live, does he have a phone number?" coaxed Hilbertson.

"He moves 'round but here's his last number," she said handing him a piece of paper torn from a church bulletin. "I called and called but he don't answer."

"Mrs. Bateman, was your grandson in any kinda trouble?"

With a sad look she shook her head, "Don't know."

"Had he been acting unusual or nervous the last time you saw him?"

"He musta come into some money 'cause he had some new gold chains and gave me two hundred dollars."

"Whadda ya think?" Garland asked as they drove away.

"Looks like my informant was right. El-Shawn was skimming and now he's probably dead."

"Yep."

"Tracking down his women'd probably be a waste of time and we're just too short of manpower."

"Yeah, he'll probably wash up somewhere along the Chattahoochee."

"He might, but have you noticed how over the last coupla years guys like him have vanished into thin air?"

"Seems to be a trend, but you know how this type can move around. They mighta gotten in trouble or had too many warrants and decided it was easier to go over to Birmingham or even New Orleans and lay low for a while."

7

EVERY WEEK DURING the spring semester Dalton's last class on Tuesday ended at three o'clock. He typically drove to Whitby to visit his elderly grandparents at an assisted living facility. They both were now in their mid-eighties and no longer capable of operating their cattle ranch. They had rented their home to a young couple who acted as caretakers of the property. Many of the pastures had been rented to nearby ranchers.

Dalton frequently took them small gifts such as bowls of fruit, trays of Genn's muffins, or flowers. But this time the car carried something extra, something he wouldn't show Genn or his grandparents. In a plastic bag in the back of the Tahoe rested a human head. Not a real head but a life-sized plastic man's head purchased from an online vendor. This head was paintable. Using some old cans of spray paint from his garage he had sprayed the head an ashy grey, the color of a corpse. He had sprayed the hair black and even used a Sharpie to blacken in the nostrils. *Genn'll think I'm insane if she finds out about this.*

Lucas Greenleigh and Margaret Beaufort Randolph occupied a pleasant cottage at Orchard Park Homes on the outskirts of town. Although his grandparents missed their former home and property and often expressed a desire to return, Dalton appreciated the amenities such as a maid service, prepared meals, and twenty-four-hour security.

"Luke, it's Dalton," exclaimed Margaret as she opened the door. "Where's your sweet wife?"

"She stayed to help some of her grad students with a charity project—prom dresses for low-income high school students."

"She's such a kind person," said Luke.

"That's one reason I married her Grandpa. Oh, she sent these dewberries. Those plants y'all gave us a few years ago are really beginning to produce."

"Some of those will go great in the fruit salad I'm making tomorrow," said Margaret. "Can you stay and eat with us tonight in the dining hall? Banana pudding is on the menu."

"That sounds so good Grandma, but I'm trying to stay on a diet plus I'm going to drop by the farm in a little while to see how things are. Genn and I are meeting at Lundigan's at seven thirty for dinner. But I can stay until about five o'clock. Grandpa, I have something I want to ask you about."

"What's that son?" he asked as they sat down.

"Sherwyn told me about the old Faustin Place—Saint-Cyr. I was wondering if you knew much about what happened there. I'd never heard of it before."

"Well, not many of your generation know that story or rather tall tale. It was talked about for so long that only the Lord knows the truth. Over the years most of the old families moved away or died out. Plus the Faustins all died off around the time of the Civil War or just afterwards."

"Sherwyn told me Faustin beat a slave to death and

41

that he disappeared just before going to prison. He also said voodoo might have been involved."

"When we were kids back in the Depression and Second World War, stories would go around about that place being haunted and there being a voodoo curse. Some banker from Birmingham owned the place back then but we kids stayed away. He had 'posted' signs up everywhere back when most people didn't care if you went on their property as long as you latched the gates behind you and didn't let out the cows. It seemed like we explored almost everywhere except that place. We made up all kinds of stories. I can still remember when the old house burned—never saw so much smoke in all my life."

"Sherwyn said something about the banker losing the property in a poker game?"

"Yeah, that's what I always heard. Anyway old Burl Hickam came to own it. He kept up the posted signs. He was a bad lot—did a lot of gamblin' and fightin' in his younger years but later became a bootlegger."

"He had a still out there?"

"Naw, he brought in bonded stuff when the county was dry back in the fifties and sixties. He probably smuggled it in from Mississippi or Louisiana. He supplied places like the Whitby Country Club and a lot of the country stores that used to be everywhere back then. He also had a gambling operation set up at each store."

"Like card games or dice?"

"This was under-the-counter stuff like punch boards and numbers, mostly black folks played those. During football season there'd be grid cards with a hundred squares. You'd pick a square for a dollar, then before the game each column would be assigned a number from zero to nine. The numbers across would be the last digit of one team's score, the numbers up and down would be the last digit of the other team's score. The winner on each card would get ninety dollars and Burl and the store would split the ten. When there was a big game like Alabama and Auburn, the squares would be ten dollars each with the winner gettin' nine hundred dollars."

"Did you ever win?"

"Coupla times I won the small pots, but your Grandma didn't approve."

"You shoulda seen the hurt look on his face when I made him put that money in the collection plate at church," said Margaret with a smile. "But you know exploitin' poor people was a big racket. Most of those bets were charged, of course if someone won, they almost never got cash, but credit on their account. Many of those folks never were able to pay off their bills. Plus a lot of the country people couldn't read or do simple math. At some of those places they'd get shortchanged if they paid in cash or overcharged if they put something on their account."

"Does that still go on?"

"Probably, but hopefully it isn't as common as it used to be. There're almost no country stores left, most folks can get to town now."

"What about the bootlegging?"

"Back then it seemed like every couple of years there'd be a referendum to legalize alcohol and the County Baptist Association would run a big campaign against it," said Luke. "The joke was that Burl was their biggest financial backer— now that was an unholy alliance."

Dalton chuckled at the thought of Baptist preachers and a bootlegger finding common cause.

"When the county went wet back in the late seventies, Burl was outta the liquor business. But he stayed on out there—became a recluse. He died a few years ago. I think his nephew, that Wellton kid, who went to prison, inherited it."

"Yeah, I remember him. He went to middle school with Genn and me, but dropped out later when he turned sixteen."

"Dalton, why are you curious about that place?"

"A while back Genn and I were driving back from the Fish Camp late in the afternoon. The sun came out just as we got to that place and I stopped to take some pictures. When I got to lookin' at them later I saw something in the distance that got me curious."

"And what did you see or think you could see?"

"Grandpa, it really disturbed me. It looked like a body was lying beside the road across the pasture, a head anyway. Genn thought my eyes were playing tricks on me and Sherwyn and Lucius didn't think much of it either. Here, take a look at this print."

Luke adjusted his glasses and leaned over close to a lamp. "Just where is this thing?"

"Right here."

"My eyes ain't what they used to be, but I think I see what you're talkin' about," he said peering intensely at the image.

"Use this magnifying glass," said Margaret.

"Dalton, I'm gonna have to be honest with you. I don't think anything's there 'cept mud and shadows."

"I just wish I could be sure, Grandpa."

Margaret tilted her head towards Dalton. "That Edgar Wellton is a bad sort, just stay away from him and that place."

"Don't worry Grandma. Genn keeps the reins pretty tight. I won't do anything foolish."

"Well you listen to her. She's as smart as a whip and the best thing you ever did was to marry her."

"Grandma, you are so right!"

For the next hour they chatted and reminisced. Dalton mentioned how he and Lucius used to climb to the top of Blindman's Bluff and look for the wreck of the *Gondolier.*

"Yeah," said Luke, "we daydreamed about that old riverboat too. We used to talk about all kinda ways to get that gold. Old Pudgee Perkins thought we could use a big magnet like the ones advertised in the back of comic books."

Dalton laughed out loud. "Lucius and I used to do the same thing!"

"I told Pudgee it wouldn't work 'cause gold ain't magnetic. But he insisted it was. So we took an old horseshoe magnet and tried it on his big sister's locket. Course it didn't work. But Pudgee claimed it was brass and not gold. His sister got mad and whacked him, insisting it was gold 'cause her boyfriend gave it to her."

"What do you think Grandpa? Is there any gold down there?"

"I've thought a lot about that over the years. To be honest, I doubt it. Those gold miners, if there were really any gold miners on board, woulda had their gold in their pockets or belts or maybe locked in strong boxes. When that boiler exploded it blew off the superstructure, you know everything above the deck. That's where the passengers woulda been. They'd have been thrown all over the place. All that was left in one piece is the hull."

"Then wouldn't the gold be scattered on the bottom?"

"You've walked across smooth wet chalk before. It's slick as ice."

"Yeah, I've busted my butt a couple of times trying to walk across Gum Pond Creek in the late summer when it was almost dried up."

"Well, the bottom of that river is nothing but slick chalk and you've seen how fast the current can move on the outside of that bend. Anything on the bottom woulda been scattered way downstream a long time ago."

"Lucius and I always thought we could scuba dive down there. Maybe there's a chest or two full of gold in the hull. You know they give lessons at the University."

"Son, that's not a safe place to dive what with the wreckage and current. Besides the tow boats swing out wide making that bend. You've seen how their prop wash throws stuff everywhere. Anyone risking their life on that wreck would be a fool. It just ain't worth it!"

"That's true Grandpa, but those tales of ghosts and gold are fun."

"Well, you just take care of yourself, don't do anything foolish. Your Grandma and I don't want anything bad to happen."

Dalton was now their only descendant and heir. Luke and Margaret's older son, Dalton's Uncle Sidney, was an Army major killed in the First Gulf War in 1991. Within months Dalton's parents perished when a log truck went out of control and struck them head-on. Although he tried to suppress the idea, Dalton would one day inherit the family property which covered several square miles of the Black Belt Prairie.

As Dalton drove away, his grandmother's face clouded, "I wish he wasn't bull-headed like his father."

"I just hope Genn can keep him out of trouble."

It took only about ten minutes or so to drive from Whitby to the Randolph Place. Dalton always smiled when he saw the quarter section pasture adjacent to the highway. The herd of Black Angus cattle once nurtured by his grandfather had been supplanted by hundreds of goats. Several round hay bales sat near the fence and there were always several ongoing "king-of-the-hill" battles.

The main entrance to the property lay just beyond the goat pasture. It was quite similar to the entrance to Edgar Wellton's place. There was no browse line in the distance but a gravel drive extended in an almost straight line from the gate for nearly a mile. *The sun was lower than this when I took that other photo but this might be close enough.*

Dalton drove along until he thought he was about the same distance from the gate as the head he thought he saw on Edgar's place. He stopped and removed the plastic head from its bag. "'Alas, poor Yorick!' I'm gonna leave you by this road."

Using a print of the earlier photo, he attempted to duplicate the position of what he took to be the head protruding from the shadows. He drove back to the entrance gate and retrieved his camera. Setting its lens to zoom he again checked the print. *This looks reasonably close.* Several frames later he retrieved poor Yorick.

After an uneventful drive back to Tuscaloosa, he arrived at Lundigan's a few minutes before seven thirty. He reached to open the restaurant's door and someone bounded up the stairs behind him three steps at a time. "Wait for me!" Genn said with a laugh. "You must really be hungry!"

A hostess seated them at a window. They didn't speak but held hands across the table and took in the view towards the west of the Black Warrior River and the setting sun.

"How romantic," said someone interrupting their private moment, "the Doctors Randolph!"

"Abigail," said Dalton, "I didn't know you worked here."

"I just started a few days ago, my car needs new tires and to quote Daddy," Abigail's voice dropped about two octaves, "Abby, it's time you learned the value of a dollar, so get a job!"

"Genn, this is Abigail Wallace, one of our students and hopefully a graduate student next year. You might remember her from our party back in the fall."

"I certainly do. It's nice to see you again," said Genn with a smile. *Oh dear, not another twenty-year-old with a crush on Dalton. And the poor boy doesn't even realize it. It's a good thing she doesn't have red hair.* "Didn't you donate a lavender outfit to our prom dress drive?"

"Why yes, I did, after your husband mentioned it to our class."

"That's a very nice dress. One of our fashion students made some minor alterations so it would fit a young woman from Pickens County. Her family could never have afforded anything so nice. I've never seen anyone happier than when she put it on."

"I wore that dress to last year's formal." *And Daddy threw one of his hissy fits when he got the credit card bill.*

By the time Genn and Dalton finished eating, only a few patrons remained in the restaurant. However, the bar remained busy as they headed for the parking lot.

"How was your dinner?" asked Dalton. "Mine was excellent."

"Mine was good but a little less salt would have made it better. Little Miss Abigail spending so much time at your side asking if we needed anything became somewhat of an annoyance."

"Well, she was just 'brown-nosing' a little. But she's such a good student, she doesn't need to."

Yeah, right, thought Genn as she nodded and her mouth formed a crooked smile.

Later that evening Genn went to bed early while Dalton sat at his laptop. He accessed the dozen or so photos he had taken a few hours earlier. *Looks like I got the distance about right. Let's see how Poor Yorick played his role.*

He displayed the single photo that showed the image beyond the browse line and chose one of the Yorick photos. After cropping and minor resizing he viewed them side-by-side.

Poor Yorick played his part better than expected! Wow, no doubt at all there was a dead body lying out there that evening! This is just too far-fetched to be a random image that I'm interpreting as a human head in the sunlight with its body in the shadows. I need to get out to that spot but how?

He shut down the laptop and crept to bed. Genn lay beneath the covers and softly mumbled. "What time is it?"

"Just after midnight—sweet dreams darling."

Dalton lay quietly obsessing about the images until he drifted off. His dreams were clouded and muddled and soon forgotten the next morning.

8

MONDAY, JULY 10, 1843
WHITBY, ALABAMA

"OYEZ! OYEZ! OYEZ! Circuit Court for the Third Judicial District of the State of Alabama is now in session, Judge Toliffer Smithson presiding! All rise!" cried the bailiff.

A short, stocky man with a shock of white hair entered from a side door. The summer heat made the room seem like an oven, but Smithson moved gracefully under his heavy judicial robes.

The judge seated himself behind the bench and adjusted the black material. He extracted a small green case from his pocket and carefully opened it. With dignity appropriate to his station he unfolded a pair of wire-rimmed spectacles, fitted them atop his nose, and secured the arms behind each ear.

"Be seated," cried the bailiff.

As Smithson picked up a sheaf of papers, murmurs arose in the back of the courtroom. The judge looked over his glasses and forcefully exclaimed, "I will not tolerate whispering, talking, or outbursts during sentencing. There will be order and silence! Monsieur Faustin, rise and face the bench."

An immaculately dressed man rose from a table to the left of the bench and stood before the judge. He wore a black frockcoat with a gray waistcoat, white linen shirt, and knotted silk cravat. His almost expressionless face bore a goatee and curled moustache.

"Before this court pronounces sentence, do you have anything to say?"

"Non, votre honneur," he replied softly.

"Monsieur Faustin, I must insist that you speak English. Our British judicial ancestors of more than a century ago may have spoken an archaic form of French in court but in these modern times and in our republic we use English."

"Yes, your honor."

"Henri Faustin, a jury has found you guilty of murder in the lashing death of the slave Hercule. He was your property. However, under our legal system and the laws of the sovereign State of Alabama, in particular, those in the bonds of servitude are afforded protection from extreme, undeserved punishment such as that meted out by *your own hand*.

These laws exist to preserve our social and economic system. Apparently Hercule did nothing more than glare at you in an insolent fashion. Such an act on his part may have deserved some minor punishment or reprimand but such cruel retribution and an agonizing death constitute a criminal act of the most severe degree. You ordered him seized to a tree and you struck him so many times upon his bare back that the coroner could not count the lacerations. When such heinous acts go unpunished we risk collapse and chaos. Just look at what happened in Haiti nearly fifty years ago and more recently in Virginia—bloody rebellion!

Scores of white men, women, and children were murdered in Virginia, but in Haiti tens of thousands died. We cannot allow that to happen here. The penalty you are about to receive must serve as an example to everyone, both free and slave, that punishment must be appropriate to the misdeed."

Throughout the courtroom many heads nodded silently in agreement.

"This court hereby sentences you to sixteen years confinement in the new state prison at Wetumpka. There you will learn firsthand what it is like to toil from daylight to dark, just as your field hands do."

In the back of the courtroom a woman sobbed into a lace handkerchief.

"Earlier today, Madam Faustin pledged a tract of land, separate from your main estate, as surety. You are hereby released on bail for thirty days. Use that time wisely, put your affairs in order. At the end of that period you will surrender your person to Sheriff McCauley for transportation to prison. I am assuming that you retain some shred of honor and that as a gentleman and former officer of Napoleon Bonaparte's army, you will abide by the terms stated."

"Yes, your honor."

"Court is adjourned."

"All rise!" cried the bailiff.

As the judge exited the courtroom, the subdued crowd rose and began filing out. Most agreed with the judge's decision. Over the years many had meted out corporeal punishment to their slaves but none so cruelly as Henri Faustin.

A woman hurried down the aisle from the back of the courtroom and embraced Faustin. "Henri, mon chéri! Que ferons-nous?"

"Thérèse! ma chérie! Things will be okay. Our son has learned much, he will be able to manage our affairs. We must petition Governor Fitzpatrick to grant a pardon. I did not know what I was doing, drink clouded my judgment and I had lost at cards. Let us return to Saint-Cyr, there is much to do."

The July sun beat down upon the carriage. The black coachman gave a gentle shake to the reins. He needed no whip. The four roan horses began to trot south along the plank road toward Saint-Cyr. They knew that cool water, grain and hay, and a shady stable awaited them.

In the back of the coach Henri Faustin stared ahead as in a trance, his face partially hidden under a broad brimmed hat. Beside him, Thérèse wiped tears from her cheeks. Silence greeted them as the carriage turned from the plank road and entered Saint-Cyr. The entrance drive was bordered on both sides by lush green fields of cotton. The plants stood almost four feet high—their branches heavy with blossoms.

"Ma chérie, cotton prices may rise this year, the bad times that began with the panic back in thirty-seven are nearing an end. The London newspapers report that English textile mills may increase production later this year. With a good harvest, we might settle most of our debts."

The carriage halted in front of the mansion's steps. A young slave opened the door and offered his hand.

"Stand aside, I need no help!" He stepped out and

assisted Thérèse. Hand-in-hand they ascended the thirteen steps to the front porch of the elevated mansion.

The double doors opened and they stepped into the grand foyer. An elderly servant bowed slightly and accepted their hats and coats.

"Madam, Monsieur, refreshments await you in the parlor."

"Merci, Édouard," said Thérèse.

Upon a mahogany table sat a large silver salver bearing a crystal pitcher of iced lemonade and a plate of small sandwiches. Thérèse poured a glass of the cold liquid and offered it to Henri.

"I need brandy."

"S'il vous plaît non, Henri!" she pleaded.

He hung his head. Alcohol and absinthe, in particular, had contributed to his increasingly erratic behavior. The bright green color of the anise flavored spirit beckoned like a siren's song. *Perhaps too much wormwood caused my temporary madness.*

Late that afternoon he rode his magnificent chestnut stallion across the fields of cotton. *That's odd, where're the field hands? I'll have them all whipped! Where're my overseers?*

At Saint-Cyr field hands lived in a work camp of scores of rough lean-tos abutting a cypress swamp nearly a mile from the big house. Henri spurred his horse and galloped there, but the camp stood empty. No smoke rose from the cook shack.

"Come out you bastards!" He screamed in English. "You can't hide in that swamp, come out now or each of you gets fifty lashes!"

Only the crows replied—cawing in the distance. There

were no overseers in sight, without them he could do nothing. He returned to his mansion.

The evening meal passed in tense silence. Henri, Thérèse, and Albert, their son, dined informally at a long polished table.

Albert rose. "Maman, papa, excusez-moi, s'il vous plaît. I must see to some legal documents that arrived earlier." His parents nodded in agreement.

Later that evening, sleep evaded Henri. He arose and went downstairs to the liquor cabinet in the parlor and retrieved a tall bottle that bore—impressed in its glass—a medallion that read 'Pernoud Couvet Suisse.' *Swiss absinthe—the very best, and what an epic journey through the Alps, across my beloved homeland, over the Atlantic and Gulf of Mexico to Mobile, and then by steamer up the Tombigbee River.*

Henri uncorked the bottle and poured the dark emerald green liquid into a crystal glass. The smell of anise almost intoxicated him. He filled a perforated silver spoon with lump sugar and placed it over the glass. He slowly poured water over the sugar. Diluted and sweetened the absinthe glowed with a pale green light. *Ahhh, la fée verte—the green fairy. I'll visit Marie's cabin,* he thought, *but first several glasses will raise my spirits.*

Except for the ticking of an ormolu mantle clock, the night had been silent but he began to hear a faint, distant drumbeat. *What are those black savages doing? Is that coming from the forest behind their cabins? Why are they drumming?* Grabbing a brace of dueling pistols Henri threw open the front doors and stood at the top of the steps. The drumming was not loud, but it was unceasing. *Where are they?* He suddenly felt anxious. *We're alone without the overseers!*

Distance and trees muted the sound. Thérèse slept undisturbed as each night she liberally dosed with the mixture of alcohol and raw opium known as laudanum. Albert was a heavy sleeper who distained open windows and fresh air. He believed night air carried the disease causing vapors known as miasmas and sleeping in the moonlight induced lunacy.

The whale oil lamp in the grand entrance foyer faintly lit the steps but little else. The near full moon hung high overhead and the cedars along the entrance drive were silhouetted against the sky. He hurried down the steps and around the corner of the mansion toward one of the cabins.

"Marie, Marie," he said softly at her door. "Let me in."

The door opened and warm arms enfolded him. "Mon chéri ... mon chéri," she whispered as her lips sought his.

"Mama, Mama," a small voice came from a tiny room at the back of the cabin. "I'm scared. What's happening?"

"Shush my darling, all's well, our master's here to protect us. Go back to sleep." Marie gently closed the tiny bedroom's door.

"What's happening, where're the slaves?"

"Most of the house servants and overseers have fled. The field hands are in the forest near the swamp. They're plotting to escape back to Africa."

"Those ignorant fools! They have no idea where they are or even how to get back to the sea. Even if they got there they don't know how to sail a ship. Why, they can't speak any languages except their tribal gibberish. What will they do? Swim back to Guinea and Dahomey?"

"They intend you harm, Henri. You must leave this place!"

"I cannot abandon you, Celeste, and our unborn child."

"They intend to kill you Henri, but they will not harm Madam Faustin or the young master. Without your knowledge they have treated the field hands with kindness and medicines, especially after severe punishment. At times your son even sends them extra food and strong drink to dull their aches and pains."

"Change into warm clothes and wrap Celeste in her blanket along with my waistcoat. I'll get the carriage and we'll flee to Natchez. From there we'll take a steamer to New Orleans and then book passage on a packet ship to Veracruz. I've heard General Santa Ana is seeking French officers for the Mexican Army. We could also go to Mérida in the new Yucatán Republic. We can live openly as man and wife in either place.

"Henri, I'm frightened."

"Dress quickly and bundle Celeste. Bring your small strong box and what food you can find. Hurry while I prepare the carriage. Come to the stables as quickly as you can."

Henri had long feared a night such as this. Marie's strong box held Spanish escudos and American gold coins along with loose gemstones—their escape fund. Marie had also sewn French Napoléons and British sovereigns into the lining of Henri's waistcoat. It would be enough to sustain them comfortably until they reached safety.

Silently Henri crept across the space between the stables and Marie's cabin. The usual night sounds could not be heard. The owls were silent and the distant wolves mute, even the crickets had ceased their usual nocturne—only the drums remained.

The horses resented the disturbance of their sleep. But one in particular, a well-tempered gelding, did not protest excessively. Henri harnessed him to the carriage. *With the gold and jewels in Marie's strong box and my waistcoat we'll be safe.*

"Mama, where are we going?"

"Whisper softly sweetheart, we are going on an exciting journey to begin a new life. You will see wonderful things and we will live happily. In a few months you will even have a new brother or sister."

"Henri, are you there?"

"Hand Celeste to me. Here, Little One, bundle up in my waistcoat and lie down in the back. The night is chilly and it is several hours until dawn. Sleep well."

He shook the reins and the gelding began trotting. He guided the carriage away from the main entrance road and along a parallel field path. "We leave by the south gate away from those damn savages."

His eyes had adjusted to the darkness. Once in the open field and under the bright moon, he could clearly see the way ahead. To his left he thought he glimpsed something moving along the rows of cotton. *Either my eyes deceive me or deer are feeding out here.* He shook the reins and hastened the pace. *Only a quarter mile to go, I must not alarm Marie.*

They neared the gate. *Over there more deer*, he thought as three dark shapes moved silently.

He handed the reins to Marie. "I must open the gate." He dismounted, threw back the gate bolt, and swung it open. As he held the gate for Marie to drive the wagon through, hands reached from the row of tall cotton plants and seized him. "Let me go you devils!" he yelled as he fought to free himself. "Go Marie, flee as fast as you can, turn left down the plank road!"

Marie shook the reins and the gelding increased his speed.

"Papa, Papa!" cried Celeste as the carriage disappeared over a slight rise in the road.

Henri struggled but his arms were bound behind him. "Release me and fight like men," he tried to shout but a gag was forced over his mouth and his curses and threats became like the moans and mumbles of a mad man.

Marie and Celeste hurdled down the plank road. "Lie down darling, we're safe now. Tomorrow is the first day of our new life. Try to forget our Master. We're free now." She thought of her little strong box and Henri's waistcoat. *We can pass for white. If asked about my olive complexion, I'll say that my mother was a Spaniard. Celeste is as white as her father. We'll stay at the inn in Selma tomorrow night and sell this horse and carriage. Then we'll take the stage to Natchez and book passage to our new home—New Orleans.*

9

BELINDA BURST INTO raucous laughter. "This boring party needs resuscitation! Come on, let's dance," she shouted as her husband looked on in disgust.

Not again, he thought with a cringe.

She grabbed young Dr. Fuentes by his sleeve. Leaving his companion behind, he reluctantly followed. "You Cubans know how to dance. Let's show a few moves!"

"Actually Mrs. Dunstan, my grandparents emigrated from Spain over sixty years ago."

"Well you look like *Ricky Ricardo* to me, but you're going to find out that I'm no *Lucy*!" She laughed and ground her crotch against his leg.

"Belinda, please let's go home. You've had too many," said her husband grasping her shoulder in an attempt to pull her from the dance floor.

"I'm just having fun with 'Little Ricky.'"

"Ma'am, my name is Joseph."

Dr. Dunstan gave his wife a stony stare. This wasn't the first time she had publically humiliated him. "Belinda, you've had too much to drink, please calm down. This is an engagement party. Don't ruin it for the young couple.

Remember what happened at the art museum reception last month? The cost of that vase was outrageous."

"Those stupid people put it on a pedestal and that party bored me more than this one!" she screamed in his face.

Dr. Dunstan's arm tightened around her shoulder. "Joe, help me get her to the car."

As they exited the room, Dr. Dunstan nodded slightly to an expressionless security man standing beside the door.

Not again, why can't I stop myself? I always have too many, now Dan's gonna be pissed. But I'm NOT going to that damn rehab place again, screw those bastards.

"It's too damned early to go home!" Belinda's slurred speech echoed through the parking deck as she tried to twist away from her husband's grasp. But he and his young partner held on tightly and half-forced her into a maroon 1968 Bristol 410 and partially reclined the seat.

"Joe, I'm so sorry, that round of rehab she finished in March didn't last long."

"It's okay Dr. Dunstan."

Dr. Joseph Fuentes stood watching as the Bristol pulled slowly away and disappeared down the exit ramp. *I don't know how he does surgery five days a week and then puts up with her. I'll remain a bachelor, thank you very much!*

Dunstan pulled out and headed south. He stared ahead stoically as they drove over Red Mountain into Homewood.

"Dan, I'm so sorry," she tried to say. But her tongue felt thick and everything seemed to be moving. "I don't want to go to sleep yet," she mouthed. But her words were inaudible. She could feel the soft leather upholstery of her seat and armrest. She slumped to the right, her head resting against the window. She felt a soft vibration as the car accelerated and she lost consciousness.

Harden your heart, this ends tonight.

He drove south on U.S. Highway 31 and then up Shades Mountain into Vestavia Hills, an affluent suburb of Birmingham, Alabama. Just over the crest he turned onto a residential street heavily lined with trees and bushes. Another vehicle followed about two hundred yards behind. Ahead a real estate agent's sale sign marked a vacant house. He drove up the driveway and stopped where his car could not be seen from the street. A black Ford Explorer pulled up beside him.

"She's passed out," he whispered.

Two men from the SUV pulled on latex gloves, laid a body bag on the ground, and unzipped it. They gently extracted Belinda Dunstan from the Bristol and laid her in the open bag. A young woman about Belinda's build and height and wearing an identical black cocktail dress exited the Explorer. The men removed the unconscious woman's jewelry and watch and handed them to her. She put them on and got in beside Dr. Dunstan.

One of the men pulled out a small gas cylinder attached by hose to a transparent mask. He fitted the mask over Belinda's mouth and nose and slipped the elastic strap behind her head. A soft hiss could be heard as he slowly opened the valve.

After a few moments, he tucked the bottle under Belinda's arm and zipped up the bag. The men slid the bag in the back of the SUV. Dunstan handed them a thick clasp envelope sealed with tape.

"Without a trace?"

"Without a trace," whispered the man with a nod.

How ironic, almost eighty percent of what we breathe is nitrogen. Make it closer to a hundred and we're in trouble.

Dunstan drove in silence. His wife's double lay slumped in the passenger's seat as they returned to his mansion. *Hafta be quiet and keep my eyes closed. Speak only when spoken to, ask no questions, and do not look at him. We mustn't be able to identify each other or recognize each other's voice.*

Dunstan turned into his six-car garage and the door closed behind him.

"No need to act drunk now," he whispered. "The servants have the night off. Take the stairs and stay in the suite to the left. Be sure to put the jewelry on the dressing table tray. Breakfast will be delivered to your door at eleven o'clock. You won't see me again as I'll be leaving early in the morning. You know the rest."

As the Explorer headed south, Belinda Dunstan lay prone in her plastic shroud. Her respiration and pulse slowed and stopped. The electrical activity in her heart and brain faded away. She wouldn't be the "life" of any more parties.

The Explorer turned west seeking the backroads of north Shelby and Bibb Counties. The men sat in silence and peered ahead into the darkness, their faces faintly illuminated by the dashboard display. Vestavia Hills lay over an hour behind as they crossed Tuscaloosa County on a series of backroads.

"Watch your speed," the passenger said. "They don't put many cops on the roads out here at night but there's no need to take chances. We're in no hurry."

After skirting Tuscaloosa, the SUV turned south. In less than an hour they were on Alabama Highway 95, the lights of Whitby glowing faintly above the treetops behind them as they entered the rolling prairie lands.

"Up ahead, a little past this bridge ... turn left on that gravel turnout." The car stopped in front of a gate. The man on the passenger side stepped out. After looking carefully each way he knelt in front of the car and within seconds the gate swung open. With lights off, the car drove through and he locked the gate behind them. The faintly visible road lay ahead. The driver cautiously crossed the field and the little stream lined with trees.

"Stop here." The man on the passenger side exited as the driver popped the hatch. The interior and brake lights had been disabled manually with a switch hidden beneath the dashboard. The man pulled the body bag from the rear of the SUV and dragged it onto the grass. He unzipped the bag, removed the face mask and empty tank, and slid Belinda Dunstan's body onto the ground. After carefully folding the bag, the man stuffed it into a heavy-duty garbage bag along with a brick and wrapped it with duct tape. At mid-channel the nearby Tombigbee River was nearly thirty feet deep. The weighted bag would be dropped from a bridge in a few minutes.

Headlights appeared along the highway. Although it was nearly half a mile away, they instinctively squatted besides the Explorer as the car passed out of sight.

"Turn 'round, let's go home." After the gate was closed and locked, the car's internal lights were reactivated and the headlights turned on. They drove across the river and returned to Birmingham by a different route.

Daniel Dunstan grew up in Ensley, a large neighborhood adjacent to Birmingham's most heavily industrialized areas. His father worked at the sprawling U.S. Steel Fairfield Works while his mother kept books for a furniture store. Dunstan dreamed of rising above his family's blue collar status and gaining the means to acquire the material things and recognition he desperately craved. At that time Ensley High School was one of the best in the state. He excelled in science, especially chemistry and biology.

Late afternoons and Saturdays Dunstan worked at a garage. Because of his manual dexterity and curiosity about how mechanical things worked, he excelled at auto repair. He spent his few free moments browsing automobile and sports car magazines displayed at a next door corner drugstore. Certain cars struck him as particularly unique and beautiful and he felt compelled to one day own them. Once he finished medical school, completed his internship and residencies, and established a lucrative private practice he had attained the means to fulfill his adolescent dreams. He prized a maroon 1968 Model 410 Bristol above all else. Some of the finest craftsmen in England built fewer than a hundred, and only a handful like his were equipped with left-hand drive. In a nod to convenience, later models such as this one utilized Chrysler V8 engines. Dunstan reveled in its power and took pride in personally maintaining it. His next purchases were a 1962 supercharged Studebaker Avanti and a 1963 split-rear-window Corvette Stingray. His very first car, a 1959 Volkswagen Karmann Ghia convertible purchased when he was an undergraduate, had been adopted by Belinda. She wanted more power so he swapped the anemic sixty horsepower four-cylinder for a Porsche engine.

The VW now had a top speed in excess of a hundred and sixty miles per hour as opposed to its original seventy-five. His small collection helped relieve the almost unending tedium of his surgical practice. He wished he had chosen his wife as carefully as his cars. For him repairing classic cars offered more gratification than repairing people. He could never junk one of his cars.

For everyday driving Dr. Dunstan preferred an emerald-green Mercedes S-Class sedan while Belinda often drove a Mercedes GL-Class SUV for shopping or extended forays around town. However, for non-work events Dr. Dunstan relished the feel of his Bristol. He especially enjoyed the stares and questions by people who had no idea what it was. Belinda used the Karmann Ghia for trips to their club and loved long drives in the country with the top down. Few younger drivers had ever seen one and many a jaw dropped when Belinda opened it up on the highway.

Belinda Dunstan's suite amazed Kicky Harris. Never had she seen such luxury. She would be staying here for over fifteen hours. So far Dunstan's face remained a mystery and it would be impossible to identify him. In fact she had no inkling of his identity. She was confident he hadn't seen her and without speaking he never heard her country accent.

Fastidiously she avoided leaving any physical evidence. Earlier that day she carefully shaved her body and a net covered her hair underneath a blond wig. She kept the wig positioned so the small tattoo behind her left ear couldn't be seen. She turned back the covers of the king size bed and rumpled the sheets and pillows. In the corner sat a leather lounge chair, she would sleep—or try to sleep—on it.

An entire wall of the bedroom seemed to be a gigantic window. *Wow, what a view, there's nothing like this where I come from!*

In fact Kicky had no idea where she was except it was somewhere near Birmingham. Her family never traveled during her childhood and she had only vague ideas of the urbanized parts of Alabama.

A vast glittering valley lay before her. Stars and planets shone brightly in the extraordinarily clear and moonless sky. A small white telescope mounted atop a tripod stood beside the window. She pulled on latex gloves and peered through the eyepiece at the scene stretching to the horizon in all directions. To her left blue lights blinked beside a busy highway—*wreck or speeding ticket?*

Straight ahead on the other side of the valley, floodlights illuminated a giant figure atop a pedestal. She had never heard of Vulcan, Roman god of the forge, who overlooked Birmingham while mooning folks in Homewood and the other suburbs behind him. She smiled. *He's bare-assed—not bad looking buns!*

Red blinking lights moved slowly across the sky—*those must be airplanes landing or taking off from the airport.*

Stepping away from the window she removed the jewelry and placed the pieces on the tray sitting atop the dressing table. *Wonder if these pearls are real? Nice little watch and earrings, but nothing I would wear.*

She took off the black cocktail dress and draped it across the chair at a small writing table. She found Belinda's underwear drawer and removed panties and a bra then dropped them in the dirty clothes hamper. The maid probably wouldn't notice they were clean. She found a bathrobe and put it on. *This'll be comfortable to sleep in,* she thought as she lay down on the lounge chair. *It's gonna be a boring night if I can't fall asleep.*

She lay in silence. No sounds emanated from the house except a faint, almost inaudible hiss as the mansion's HVAC system turned on. Her mind raced. *It's for sure they killed that woman, now I'm an accessory to murder! I shouldn't have let my boyfriend talk me into this! What am I gonna do if I get caught? I need my medicine but they wouldn't let me bring any. Damn, I'm hungry, wish I had eaten during the day. And now I hafta pee!*

After using Belinda's bathroom she sprayed the toilet and sink with a diluted bleach cleanser she found under the sink. She had been warned to scrupulously avoid leaving any trace that might yield DNA. Upon leaving the bathroom Kicky looked back in amazement. She had never seen marble floors and walls and gold plated fixtures.

Stress and anxiety leading up to the evening robbed her of sleep for several nights. The overwhelming fatigue and drive to the mansion drained her to the point of exhaustion. She almost immediately fell asleep.

10

A GLOW ON the eastern horizon announced the impending dawn. A mockingbird sang and in the distant woods a pileated woodpecker intermittently drummed on a hollow tree. Edgar awoke and lay listening.

Did they come last night? He sat on the edge of his bed and pulled on his boots. No need to dress, he had slept in his work clothes.

His truck started with a roar and he drove toward the front of his property. He topped a high spot and there beside the road lay a body.

Who was she, where did she come from, and who brought her here? He always wondered but clearly understood that the less he knew the better. A middle-aged woman with blond hair lay face up clothed in an expensive looking black dress. *Unusual, most of the time it's some black dude with a bullet in the back of his head.*

Her body showed no signs of violence. It seemed as if she simply fell asleep under the stars. She had been stripped of any jewelry or watch. Of course decomposition would eventually erase her features and fingerprints. His friends simply wanted the bodies to vanish. Just another missing person who would be forgotten as the years passed—*no corpse, no crime.*

A plastic bag stuffed with small bills was pinned to her dress. Edgar slipped it into the bib of his overalls and gently lifted her onto the truck bed. Until now he had had no feelings for the persons whose bodies were left on his property. However, this woman was about the age his mother would have been and he felt she deserved some degree of dignity.

Usually he tied a rope around the corpse's feet and pulled it onto the bed of his truck, but not this time. He drove about a hundred yards and stopped beside a gnarled and ancient bodock tree. Beneath it lay a battered sheet of rusty tin roofing. He cautiously pulled it aside. Once a large rattlesnake had taken up residence—*God, I hate snakes!*

This time no reptiles lurked there, only a few spiders and a hole in the ground about two feet across. He lifted her stiff body and slid it headfirst down the hole. He heard a faint thump as she hit the bottom. He took a sack of hydrated lime from his truck and dumped a good part of it down the hole.

That was easy, just like the others. He patted the bag of cash in his pocket. *Good way to start the day,* he thought with a smile. *Better go back and clean up. Hafta be at work by seven and don't forget to wash out the truck bed!* He never went to church but nonetheless hated going to the garage on Sunday.

Each day Edgar arose before dawn to see if a delivery had arrived during the night, except once the month before. Late one Friday afternoon his boss asked him come in the next day and work overtime. On his way home that Friday evening he stopped at a bar outside Meridian and met a girl. He went home with her but before he could leave, the heavy rains began. She begged him to stay and he couldn't resist. Living on the old place and commuting every day was a lonely life. Saturday he went directly to the shop. *Maybe there was no delivery last night.*

He returned after dark and beyond the browse line in the mud beside the field road lay another body. It had been there through Friday night and all day Saturday. But it was unlikely anyone had seen it. After all it had rained and who would stop along the highway to look out across his property? Then again no one had eyesight sharp enough to spot a prone corpse from half a mile away on a rainy day. He disposed of the body immediately.

The drive to work usually took about forty-five minutes but often seemed less as Edgar listened to a Meridian radio station that played country music. Some mornings if he left earlier he could tune in a crazed evangelist broadcasting on an old AM station out of Houston. Edgar always cackled when the preacher offered lockets filled with mustard seeds and little vials of oil pressed from olives plucked from a two-thousand-year-old tree that once shaded Jesus. The charlatan even read letters from listeners who claimed the oil cured everything from hemorrhoids to brain tumors—if rubbed on the appropriate body part.

But this morning was different. The woman in the black dress haunted his thoughts and brought back images of his mother sitting behind him in the courtroom day after day during his trial for the murder of a man at a tavern just across the state line near Whynot, Mississippi. He didn't like the way the man grinned while staring at him.

"What are you lookin' at?" Edgar challenged.

"Absolutely nuthin," said the man with a chuckle as he turned away.

Edgar rose from his seat, grabbed the man by the shoulder, and spun him around. As he turned the man struck a glancing blow to Edgar's head. Edgar shoved him down, gripped his head, and began pounding it against the floor. People standing nearby backed away as the man struggled to get to his feet, but Edgar kept pounding. He was consumed by a rage unlike anything he had ever experienced. "The son-of-a-bitch was making fun of me!" he screamed.

Suddenly Edgar felt searing pain and then blackness. A bystander had hit him in the back of the head with a chair. But unlike saloon brawls in old western movies the chair didn't shatter, it just made a dull thud as it struck him.

He awoke several hours later with the worst headache of his life. Two Lauderdale County Sheriff's Deputies loomed over him. "Edgar Wellton, you're under arrest for the murder of Lawson Tomlinson. Read him his rights Deputy Spencer."

The next days were a painful blur. In spite of a severe concussion he wasn't admitted to a hospital, but instead sat in jail. A judge set his bail at fifty thousand dollars. But there was no one to pay it. His mother was penniless and who would want to bail him out anyway.

It took nine months for the case to reach trial. Most of the witnesses claimed they didn't see the altercation. Others were too intoxicated and the few that did testify gave conflicting testimony. The case finally went to the jury and after nearly two days of deliberation they found Edgar guilty of a lesser charge—manslaughter. At the sentencing hearing the judge gave Edgar twelve years—twelve years at Parchman Farm.

Parchman proved to be everything he had heard at the Meridian jail. "Watch yourself, be careful, and don't talk too much," his fellow prisoners had said.

He shared a cell with someone from Noxubee County, Mississippi, a Black Belt county much like Big Tom. Grumpy Dickinson was nicknamed for the Disney character Grumpy from the movie *Snow White*. But Grumpy Dickinson wasn't a dwarf. He was just several inches shorter than average and considerably older than Edgar. Years of working out with weights had given him a muscular physique that made his shoulders appear to be as wide as he was tall.

Although they did not become friends at first, they became comfortable with the presence of each other. They talked about their lives back home and found that although of different races their stories were remarkably similar— poverty, neglect, abuse. Grumpy said his family had to haul water in barrels before the county water system reached their remote home. Edgar said in the old days in the Black Belt rich people dug enormous cisterns that caught rainwater running off roofs, and how one of the old cisterns was on his uncle's farm.

A few months later an assistant warden summoned Edgar to his office. "Wellton, have a seat, I have some difficult news. Sheriff Mosby from Tombigbee County called this morning. Your mother died several days ago."

Edgar was stunned. He felt lightheaded and his chest seemed to be collapsing.

"My mother's dead? But she's only fifty years old."

"I'm very sorry Wellton. She was found in her housing

project apartment in Whitby. Her neighbors became concerned when she wouldn't come to the door. The manager went in and she was dead on a couch. Sheriff Mosby thinks it was an overdose, but they won't know for sure until after the post-mortem.

Edgar stared stoically at the man opposite him. "I know the rules."

"We don't have any flexibility in a situation like this. You have to remain here. Would you like to talk to one of the chaplains?" Edgar shook his head. "Is there anything you want me to pass along to the folks over there?"

"Yeah, just one thing, don't bury her next to my father."

"Man, that's tough," said Grumpy sympathetically. "I remember how it was when my mama died. We all take that kinda thing differently so I can't say 'I know how you feel.' But I am sorry."

Over the next few days several inmates Edgar knew only casually expressed sympathy. They even gave him several packs of cigarettes, some packaged snacks, and a sheet of stamps—valuable prison commodities. For once in his life people other than his mother treated him with kindness. They began including him in recreational activities and even asked him to sit with them at meals.

Finally, thought Edgar, *I have friends.*

11

KICKY HARRIS AWOKE with a start. *Where am I? What time is it?* Her eyes found the bedside clock. *Almost eleven, gotta start gettin' ready.*

The cook delivered a breakfast tray to her door at the usual time, announcing its arrival with gentle rapping. She ate sparingly and placed the tray back on the hallway table.

With one exception, she resisted the temptation to browse through Belinda Dunstan's belongings. She carefully opened the doors of a magnificent built-in rosewood jewelry cabinet. *Mustn't touch!* But the urge was too strong. She had never seen so many fine things. She pulled open a drawer filled with myriad rings. The cabinet's internal lights created a dazzling display. One large diamond ring in particular mesmerized her. The center stone was the largest she had ever seen.

Could this possibly be real? There's so much stuff here, it won't be missed. They'll probably think she was wearing it when she disappeared. It won't hurt to try it on—oh my, it fits perfectly!

She removed the latex glove and slid the ring on her bare finger. Instantly she felt a rush as good as any injected drug. *She's dead. What the hell difference does it make? This ring's mine now!* She pulled the glove back on her hand and over the ring.

In the early afternoon she changed into one of Belinda's casual outfits, covered her blond wig with a silk scarf, and her eyes with a pair of Tiffany sunglasses. Promptly at one thirty she went to the garage and found the keys and a single page of directions in the Karmann Ghia's glove compartment. *Interesting, hope my truck's there.*

She started the convertible—*nice sounding engine*— opened the garage door, and drove away leaving a video record of her departure on the mansion's security system. She turned left onto Shades Crest Drive and drove past what seemed to be an endless row of the most expensive homes she had ever seen. *Well, how about that? Not a single mobile home or junk pickup in sight.*

After a few minutes she came to an intersection with U.S. 280—the busiest highway she had ever seen—and turned right. Even though it was Sunday, almost bumper-to-bumper traffic swept her past mile after mile of businesses, office parks, motels and restaurants. At one traffic light, a pickup topped with a rack of ladders pulled beside her. She glanced to her right and a man with three front teeth missing leered at her with a broad grin. Expressionless she stared ahead and as the light turned green, roared away. *This little car can almost fly!* She glanced in the mirror and ladderman, the toothless wonder, rapidly disappeared.

At tiny Harpersville, she turned right on Alabama Highway 25. The countryside looked familiar and comfortable. Modest brick homes and double-wide trailers sat scattered along the way. In places over-arching tree branches almost turned the road into a leafy tunnel. Sunlight shone through and gently flickered over her as she drove along. She passed through small towns—Wilsonville, Columbiana, Calera, Montevallo, Wilton, Centreville and Brent—all vaguely familiar as she had only seen them as names on an old highway map in the glove compartment of her truck.

South of Brent, the road forked with Highway 25 veering right, but she continued straight ahead on what was now Highway 5. Dense forests lined the road, only a few homes could be seen. She left Bibb County behind and crossed into north Perry County. In minutes she drove through Heiberger, a rural community of scattered homes. Just beyond, she turned onto a private single lane dirt drive and entered a dense pine forest. She closed a gate behind her and drove perhaps a quarter mile. She came upon a rusting metal shed housing battered logging equipment. She pulled in and parked between an ancient log truck and her old pickup. *This whole thing's been carefully planned. How did they arrange for my truck to be here?* On the seat she found a pair of her blue jeans and a tee shirt. After changing, she stuffed her disguise into the Karmann Ghia's trunk. *I've never seen a car with its trunk in the front!* She left the keys in the ignition.

Kicky drove out the other side of the shed and returned to the highway. Further down the road she reached under the driver's seat and removed a Ziploc bag containing more directions and 100 twenty-dollar bills—*not bad for a day's work, plus I got this ring!*

Soon she drove into Greensboro and turned onto Alabama Highway 69—a route she knew well. She drove north through Moundville, Tuscaloosa, Northport, and Oakman. The sun began to set as she stopped in front of a rented trailer in north Walker County. *What's gonna happen to that little car? Wish I coulda kept it. It sure was fun to drive!*

Kicky's boyfriend met her at the door. Benjamin recruited her for this charade and had been her only contact. He also kept her generously supplied with her favorite medication. After a smile and a kiss he discretely handed her a bag containing several vials of fentanyl and disposable syringes.

Back in the forest in Perry County, the Karmann Ghia lay buried in a pit beneath a thick stand of young pines. The fill dirt and topsoil were firmly compacted over it and the pine straw carefully replaced. In a few weeks the area would appear natural and undisturbed.

Kicky Harris grew up in a house trailer in a dilapidated mobile home park in Walker County, Alabama. She showed considerable promise in high school and became the first member of her family to go to college. As a freshman at the University of North Alabama in Florence she felt isolated and socially inept. Her heavy country accent and unfashionable clothes embarrassed her. She avoided going home so most weekends were spent alone as making friends proved difficult. However, in the fall of her sophomore year she met Benjamin. Being somewhat of a loner too, she felt drawn to him. After a few study dates and trips to the campus coffee shop she confided some of her social anxieties to him.

"No problem," he said. "Take one of these, it'll smooth things out." Indeed she became more relaxed, even euphoric.

Benjamin made her feel special, pretty, and confident.

But these feelings persisted only with the help of more of Benjamin's "prescription."

"Some friends are partying tonight."

"I'm not sure I want to go," she said with some reluctance. "Got a paper due in the morning and I need to study for midterms."

"There'll be sumthin special. Come on. You'll see."

Kicky didn't like needles. Vaccinations for childhood diseases terrified her as a child. Her mother had to restrain her as the nurse struggled to hit the flailing target.

"It's okay," he whispered. "Your skin's thin so it won't hurt." She looked away as he slipped the needle into the vein in the crook of her arm. Within seconds she could feel the opiate take effect.

"Umm," she purred. "I feel so good. Let's go to that back bedroom."

12

"VESTAVIA HILLS POLICE Department, how may I direct your call?"

"Yes please, I'd like to talk to someone about filing a missing person report."

"One moment please."

"Detective Maddingley."

"This is Daniel Dunstan. My wife, Belinda, has been missing since last night."

"What makes you think she's missing?"

"She left yesterday afternoon at about one thirty and never returned. I've tried her cell phone and contacted some of her friends. The calls roll over to voice mail and no one has seen or heard from her. That's very out of character. I'm really concerned."

"Mr. Dunstan, I suggest that you come by our office. We usually don't start an investigation right away, until there's some obvious cause for concern. Sometimes people just want to get away or drop out of sight for a while. Are there any medical, mental, substance abuse, or relationship issues?"

"No, not that I know of, although she did go through

rehab for an alcohol problem just a couple of months ago. This is so unlike her."

"Are any of her things missing? What about her car? These are just some of the things that have to be considered."

"Well, I'm a physician, a surgeon actually, and I just finished a couple of early morning procedures. Actually any time this afternoon or in the morning after nine will be fine. I can easily clear my schedule."

"In that case my partner and I can come to your office. How about after lunch, say around two."

"That'll be great, thank you for responding so quickly," said Dunstan.

"If you hear from her in the meantime please call us promptly," said Maddingley as they ended the call.

Dunstan, Dunstan, where have I heard that name? His partner came in from the break room with coffee and a donut. "Hey Peggy, have you ever heard of Dr. Daniel Dunstan and his wife, Belinda?"

"Yeah, they're big socialites. Dunstan's an über wealthy surgeon, far richer than most doctors. Rumor is he made his big bucks in real estate. Years ago he bought a large farm just off 280 in north Shelby County for his wife's horses. But a hospital board decided it was ideal for a new medical complex and paid millions for part of it. Some real estate trust has been developing the rest. You know a new golf course and multi-million dollar homes. What's the deal?"

"Dunstan says his wife's been missing since yesterday afternoon."

"Maybe she ran off with her tennis instructor or the pool boy. I understand they don't have children and she doesn't work so she's got lots of time on her hands. They're in the society rags all the time—charity balls, fundraisers—you know all tans, toothy smiles, and upraised glasses for the camera. In recent years his wife developed a reputation for being a lush who's logged lots of affairs. They live in a big mansion just off Shades Crest. Earlier this year she got drunk at an art museum fundraiser and smashed a rare René Lalique vase. Insurance doesn't cover that sorta thing. I heard Dunstan had to shell out a high five-figure amount. The museum put spin on the incident by labeling it an unfortunate accident, but I heard from one of the event planners that she actually snatched it off a pedestal and threw it at him. You'd think sumthin that valuable would be under glass."

"That's very interesting. I hafta be the only cop in America whose partner has degrees in decorative art history and criminal justice along with knowledge of current society gossip."

"Unless she's run off and left the good doctor, sumthin serious must have happened—accident, carjacking, whatever. By the way, Chief brought several boxes of Krispy Kremes this mornin' … you'd better go get one before they're all gone. There's a fresh pot of coffee and yum, these are great crullers!"

Reardon pulled their unmarked car into the parking deck of a medical office building on Birmingham's Southside. The reflective glass panels covering it mirrored the nearby buildings, the sparse trees, and sky. *I don't like modern architecture but at least this big ugly box is partially camouflaged.*

They exited the elevator on the fifth floor and on the opposite wall stainless steel letters announced "Dunstan

Surgical Associates LLC, Dr. Daniel Dunstan, Dr. Joseph Z. Fuentes, Dr. Elizabeth Penrith, Dr. Alton Pendleton, III."

A smiling receptionist rose to greet them as they showed their IDs. She spoke into her headset microphone. "Dr. Dunstan your two o'clock is here."

Reardon looked around the reception area. *Understated, but nice, better than most I've seen.*

"Please follow me," she said leading them down a short corridor. She tapped gently on a partially open door. A man of medium height and build wearing a long white lab coat came to the door. He appeared to be middle-aged and was clean-shaven. He did not smile and seemed anxious.

"Come in, I'm Daniel Dunstan," he said offering his hand.

"Good afternoon, Dr. Dunstan. This is Detective Peggy Reardon and I'm Detective Clayton Maddingley."

"Nice to meet you both, please have a seat."

The detectives sat in soft leather chairs facing Dunstan's huge antique walnut desk. Maddingley glanced around the spacious office. *Wish I had this chair back at the office.*

Reardon noticed two small landscape paintings in ornate gilded frames. *Those have to be by Corot, easily forty thousand each.*

"Sir, we've already started the investigation into your wife's disappearance," said Maddingley. "We'd like to begin this interview by going over the events of this past weekend, please describe what transpired those two days."

"I was busy at a free clinic most of Saturday. I believe Belinda relaxed most of the day. Then we attended an engagement party Saturday night. Sunday I played golf while Belinda slept late and went for a drive."

"Tell us about your activities at the free clinic," said Maddingley.

"It's over in West End. Our church and several others sponsor it. I do this once a month. Since I'm a surgeon, I typically do fairly simple outpatient procedures—you know things such as follow up exams on patients who've had major operations, checking scars and wounds, removing stitches and staples, etc. My PA could do most of those things, but I prefer the personal one-on-one contact. For me one of the problems with being a surgeon is that your patients are unconscious most of the time you're with them so these Saturdays are a nice break from routine."

"Was Saturday a busy day?" asked Maddingley.

"I'd say it was typical. I went in at around seven and saw, I believe, about a dozen or so patients. These people are all indigent—some even homeless. I try to spend at least twenty to thirty minutes with each. Usually the procedures take only a few moments. But most of them are lonely, depressed, and even mentally ill. I try to make them feel that someone is concerned about their welfare."

"What did you do for lunch? And what time did you leave?"

"I finished with the patients around one. The clinic operates in conjunction with a soup kitchen. I like to eat a little something with our clients and then take time to circulate and chat with them. I believe I left sometime after two."

"Did you go directly home?" asked Reardon looking over the top of her glasses and up from her legal pad.

"Yes, I did. I spent a few hours in the garage. I have several vintage cars that I enjoy maintaining. I changed the oil in one and did some minor things to the others—checked batteries and tires. Then idled them for a while. Oh, yeah, I also cleaned up the Bristol since Belinda and I were going to an engagement party that evening."

"I don't believe I've ever heard of a Bristol," said Maddingley cocking his head with a slightly puzzled look.

"They're built by hand in England. Mine is a '68, has a small-block Chrysler V8 and is easy to service. It's quite a comfortable drive. I like to use it on special occasions, social functions, that sorta thing."

"What do you and your wife usually drive?"

"For everyday use we have a pair of Mercedes. I modified my old VW Karmann Ghia convertible from college. I gave it a Porsche 911 engine and transmission, new electrical system, and heavy-duty suspension and brakes. In nice weather Belinda takes it on short trips or maybe even long drives in the country, but only when she can keep the top down. Karmann Ghia tops can be difficult to raise or lower by yourself. So if she got caught in a sudden shower, she'd be soaked."

"Tell us about her drives in the country," said Reardon. "Where did she usually go?"

"She says she sometimes has the need to get away and will go for a long drive—maybe down in Shelby County or over towards Mount Cheaha. She really loves high places that have views out across the countryside. The architect who designed our house made that a major feature of our bedrooms. Both have nice views out across Shades Valley."

"Where else might she have gone?"

"Sometimes she drives west on Shades Crest and then towards Bibb County. She usually doesn't talk much about where she goes, except the areas I mentioned. She grew up on a farm in Lawrence County on the edge of the Tennessee Valley and misses rural life—especially open countryside and forests. But she has no immediate family left up there and the farm changed hands years ago. There are several cousins in that area but I don't think she has much contact with them."

"Were there any other spots she was drawn to besides the ones you've already told us about?"

"Well, she likes Lovers' Leap over in Bluff Park and Bald Rock at Mount Cheaha. There're some spots on Oak Mountain she used to go to but she complained there were too many people."

"Tell us about Saturday night," said Reardon leaning forward.

"We attended an engagement party for our neighbors' daughter. It was at a venue downtown. We arrived at about half past seven."

"How long did you stay?"

"Not long, Belinda wasn't feeling well so we left around nine."

"Was she intoxicated?"

"She probably had one too many."

"Dr. Dunstan, does your wife have a substance abuse problem?" asked Maddingley.

"To be honest she occasionally suffers from stress, especially in those sorts of situations, and sometimes drinks too much."

"Did she act inappropriately? Is that why you left early?"

"Sometimes she becomes a little too animated and can be disruptive. She's actually quite shy and sometimes overcompensates. I felt it would be best to return home. My senior partner, Joe Fuentes, helped me escort her out to the car and we returned home."

"Did you go directly home?" asked Maddingley.

"Not immediately, it was a nice evening. I drove through Homewood and along Shades Crest. The fresh air along the top of the mountain seemed to do her good. She was asleep when we got home, but I woke her up and with a little help she was able to walk up to her suite."

"Her suite?" asked Reardon with a quizzical expression.

"Yes, we have separate suites. Each of us has our own bedroom and master bath."

"Isn't that unusual?" asked Maddingley.

"Actually it works quite well in our situation. You see we have no children and Belinda doesn't work. She usually likes to sleep in until about eleven or so. The cook takes her a breakfast tray and leaves it on a hall table outside her door. On the other hand, I'm an early riser since many surgical procedures begin in the morning. Also I love golf and when possible, play a round starting early Sunday mornings."

"Is that what you did this particular Sunday?"

"The weather was perfect. I met some friends at the club at about six thirty. We actually got in two rounds. I returned home at about four."

"What about Mrs. Dunstan?"

"She was still asleep when I left. The cook told me that she saw Belinda leave at about half past one—maybe for a drive in the country—but I'm not sure."

"Did you communicate with her after that?"

"Actually I had no contact with her on Sunday at all and have heard nothing from her since. I called several times, but there's no answer, it just goes to voice mail. She often forgets to charge her phone. I became concerned Sunday night but waited to call until this morning."

"Why didn't you call Sunday night when you first became concerned?"

"Sometimes on days like Sunday she might meet up with friends and go to a movie or eat out. A couple of times in the past she's spent the night at a friend's house."

"Dr. Dunstan this is a routine question for this type of investigation. Was your wife involved in a relationship with anyone?" asked Reardon.

"I'm not sure how to answer that, but I've had suspicions in the past. Honestly, Belinda struggles with several issues. Detective, I love her very much and can forgive anything she's done. What's important is the present and the future, the past is behind us. I just want her to safely return."

"Did something happen recently at the art museum?

How the hell did they hear about that? "An unfortunate incident did occur at the opening of the French Art Deco exhibition. I said something that upset Belinda. She turned away and stumbled on the edge of a carpet and knocked over a pedestal that held up a rather expensive vase. It shattered and could not be restored. Fortunately it was from the museum's collection and not one of the pieces on loan from France. Of course we reimbursed the museum for the replacement value."

"How much did that cost?" asked Maddingley looking up from his notes.

"I'd rather not say but it was expensive."

"Were you and your wife arguing Saturday night?"

"No."

"Did she behave inappropriately in any way?"

"She sometimes teases Dr. Fuentes since he's one of the most eligible bachelors around. I think he misinterpreted her actions."

"Detective Reardon, do you have any more questions?" She shook her head.

"Dr. Dunstan, we will need several things such as the numbers of your wife's credit and debit cards, cell phone, and the VIN and description of the car," said Maddingley. "We'll begin monitoring the cards and phone and put out a BOLO for her and her convertible. Also we'll need any video if you have a home security system."

"I'll contact my accountant right way and authorize him to turn over that information. He'll also contact the security company for the video. He should call you within the next few minutes."

"I think that will be all for now. Like I said earlier, the investigation has already begun. In the meantime if you hear from her, contact us immediately."

"Thank you Detectives, I appreciate all that you and the other officers are doing. My secretary will see you out."

"He's not tellin' us everything," said Reardon through her teeth as they walked across the parking lot.

"Yeah, and I don't think she ran away with her masseur from the spa. Dunstan sure talked a lot. He was sweaty and as nervous as a potato chip on game day."

"Sounds to me like he's been coached on what to say, then said way, way too much, especially how he empathizes with the homeless. Then he brags about his cars."

This bird likes to sing but it's all about himself.

13

THE CHOPPING BLOCK café in Jasper, Alabama filled with customers as Kicky Harris passed out menus, took orders, delivered plates, and poured iced tea and water. The weekend events had exhausted her. Although she slept several hours at the mansion, she awoke unrefreshed and tense. After disposing of the convertible and returning home she began to have doubts about her role in the events of Saturday night and Sunday. She kept trying to rationalize her actions with thoughts that if she had not stood in for that woman, then someone else would have and they would have gotten the money. But her conscience kept gnawing at her. *I've done a terrible thing.* She slept fitfully that evening and was still fatigued when she went to work early Monday morning to help prep for the noon and evening meals. Now she had to hurry from table to table for hours.

Her feelings of regret faded as her feet and back throbbed. She hated putting on a fake smile and engaging in meaningless chit-chat. *I'm gonna quit soon, a few more jobs like the one Saturday and Sunday and I won't need tips anymore. Maybe that ring will bring big dollars, but I don't wanna part with it. I could quit this friggin' dump and go somewhere fun with Benjamin.*

He picked her up after the tables were cleaned, the chairs put up, and the floors mopped.

"Ben, I'm gonna quit," she said as they drove to their rented trailer. "I hate that place! There're a couple of creeps that keep hitting on me and there's always some old bitch beating me outta my tip and last week one damned idiot even grabbed my ass."

"Baby, that's a good idea—get comfortable and I'll give you your medicine." She stripped down and put on a tee shirt. He lit a cigarette and gave it to her as she laid down on a battered sofa. He got out his kit and injected fentanyl into her jugular vein.

"Put your cigarette in this ashtray before you fall asleep," he said massaging her feet. The high dose kicked in almost immediately and she closed her eyes. Benjamin slipped on latex gloves and wiped the syringe and drug vial clean and laid them on the floor. He took the lit cigarette from the ashtray and laid it on the sofa beside her. It burned slowly, initially only scorching the upholstery but soon a wisp of acrid smoke rose. Benjamin slipped the bag of twenty-dollar bills from under the cushion. He remained outside for nearly half an hour until dense smoke poured from around the door. *That should do it.*

He walked down the driveway and began hiking west. Ten minutes later an old Toyota Corolla stopped. He got in and they drove away. In a few hours he would check into a south Mississippi hotel casino.

"What's that smell?" the woman said as she sat up in bed.

"You're always a smellin' sumthin!" groused her elderly husband.

"It's not wood smoke ... it's more like burning plastic or electric wires."

"All right, I'll look outside." With back aching and knees hurting he got up. *Gettin' old is hell.* He opened the front door, and saw what looked like thin fog or haze covering the front yard across the road and a faint glow beyond. "Call nine-one-one, that old trailer over yonder is burnin' up!"

Rural fire departments aren't known for rapid response since their members have to rush from their homes and jobs. Three sleepy firefighters arrived about ten minutes later. By then the fire had exhausted the oxygen in the trailer and choked down, but it still smoldered. One of them connected to a nearby fire hydrant while the others forced the door open, entered the trailer, and found Kicky. They lifted her from the smoldering sofa and carried her outside while the other sprayed the inside of the trailer, going from room to room searching for others.

Kicky had no pulse or respiration. They started CPR and within moments an ambulance arrived. However, she never responded and the emergency room physician at Walker Baptist Medical Center pronounced her dead upon arrival.

Mona Abbington, one of the firefighters and the single mother of two teenage sons, raked the remains of the smoldering sofa looking for embers or hot spots. Among the springs and burnt upholstery something sparkled in the glare of flashing emergency lights.

What's this? She pulled off a heavy glove and gently picked it up. *Is this a toy ring from a dollar store? Nooo ... it's too heavy, it must be real! What's a druggie waitress doin' with sumthin like this?*

She glanced around. No one looked her way. She slipped the ring into a pocket and went back to work on the remains of the cheap sofa.

Returning home just after dawn she examined the ring closely. The bold initials "HW" and the hallmark stood out clearly. She turned on her laptop and searched. *Oh my! HW stands for Harry Winston and the band is eighteen-carat white gold. This thing's real and that diamond must be four or five carats at least! Woo-Hoo! No more payday loans!*

An Alabama State Fire Marshal arrived at the scene just after eight that morning. He had reviewed the scenes of countless fires and was especially vigilant for signs of insurance fraud or arson. But when a fire involved a fatality, homicide became the issue of immediate concern. His preliminary investigation indicated that Kicky Harris injected an opiate, fell asleep, and dropped a lit cigarette on her sofa. The burning upholstery produced toxic fumes and smoke that caused her death. The main evidence consisted of a syringe, an empty fentanyl vial, the remains of a pack of cigarettes, and a cigarette butt that had apparently rolled off the sofa onto the floor. The autopsy report issued a few weeks later stated that the cause of death was toxic fume and smoke inhalation and that the victim had a high level of opiates in her blood. The fire marshal ruled the death accidental.

14

AMELIA LETITIA BAKER entered the Dunstan mansion's sunroom. Two visitors stood looking out at the courtyard and the gardens below and turned to greet her.

She appeared to be in her mid-forties. She wore dark trousers with a grey top, her glasses and hairstyle giving her the appearance of a bank officer or mid-level corporate manager. She wore no jewelry except for tiny gold stud earrings and a leather strap gold watch on her left wrist. *That's a vintage Longines,* thought Reardon, *just like my mother's.*

"Good morning Ms. Baker. I'm Clayton Maddingley and this is Detective Peggy Reardon. We need to ask you some questions about the events of this past Saturday and Sunday, the fourteenth and fifteenth."

"Certainly," she said. "Let's sit around the table. Would you like some water or coffee? Ms. McCaffey is just outside, she'll be glad to bring us something." Both detectives declined the offer.

"First tell us in your own words what transpired this past weekend," said Reardon.

"It was an 'off' weekend so to speak. Dr. and Mrs. Dunstan attended an engagement party Saturday night but nothing was scheduled here at the mansion—no house guests. The Dunstans are thoughtful employers. If nothing is going on here, they usually give us Saturday afternoon and evening and Sunday morning off. This is in addition to our usual free time. I performed my duties Saturday morning. Since I'm Mrs. Dunstan's personal assistant, I always lay out her evening attire."

"Did she tell you what she planned to wear that evening?" asked Reardon.

"Sometimes she would tell me what she wanted to wear but for that occasion she asked me to choose something. She always says she likes my choices."

"What did you pick out that evening?"

"Dr. Dunstan recently gave her a beautiful black cocktail dress—a classic Halston design. He asked me to put it out for her. She always looks good in black. It really compliments her features and highlights her jewelry."

"Do you often choose her jewelry too?" asked Maddingley.

"Not usually, she has a great sense of what is appropriate. She has some very nice things but is always careful to wear only one standout piece at a time."

"Do you know what she wore Saturday evening?"

"Apparently she chose a three-strand natural pearl necklace, a gold wedding band, a vintage Piaget watch— rose gold but simple and very elegant—and small diamond drop earrings."

"If you weren't there, how do you know she wore these things?" asked Reardon.

"She doesn't put the things she's worn back in the cabinet. She lays them out on a velvet lined tray on her dressing table. After cleaning the pieces, I put them away. I keep a detailed inventory. Since her collection is insured, every piece is documented with an appraisal and most have microscopic identification numbers etched somewhere on them. I keep a spreadsheet that lists all the pieces and update it every week for insurance purposes."

"You seem to know a lot about jewelry," stated Reardon.

"Well, I worked in counter sales for a couple of years at Mendelssohn's Jewelry and developed good relationships with a number of our clients including Mrs. Dunstan. Then Mrs. Mendelssohn asked me to accompany her on buying trips and to auctions with these clients in mind. She taught me a great deal. Mrs. Dunstan even trusted me to bid on her behalf in several auctions. When Mrs. Mendelssohn retired, Belinda, and I only address her by her first name in private, asked me to become her personal assistant."

"Were her purchases extravagant?"

"Not for someone of her and her husband's resources. Many of her pieces have high value, but she's a very astute buyer—always careful about quality, value, and potential for future appreciation. Her jewelry collection is actually a marvelous investment."

"What was she wearing when she drove off and disappeared the next day?"

"When she dresses casually, she usually wears nothing but her wedding band and simple inexpensive earrings, which by the way, aren't insured."

"Earlier you mentioned that you keep a spreadsheet listing all her fine jewelry. We need a copy of it," said Maddingley.

"Certainly," said Baker.

"In your experience, did Mrs. Dunstan drink to excess?" asked Reardon.

"Mrs. Dunstan, if I may be frank, often felt out of place. I'm afraid she suffers from an inferiority complex. But of course she has no reason to feel that way. She's from a North Alabama farm family of modest means—they were wonderful people but not members of the social set. She's uncomfortable in many social situations and alcohol helps relieve her anxieties. I really empathize since my rural Mississippi background is even more modest."

"Had she been drinking that Saturday?"

"I left just after lunch. She had at least three glasses of white wine that I saw."

"Tell us about your time off."

"I left at about one that afternoon to visit my sister. She raises horses near Brooksville, south of Columbus, Mississippi. It's about two and a half hours away. We had an afternoon cookout and I returned at about ten o'clock that evening."

"We'll need your sister's phone number for verification. It's part of our investigative protocol."

"Yes, of course."

"Had the Dunstans returned by then?" asked Maddingley.

"I have no idea. My living quarters and those of the cook are in an attached wing. I had no duties until Sunday afternoon, so I attended church that morning."

"Did you see Mrs. Dunstan Sunday?"

"Only that afternoon when she left in her convertible."

"Did she speak to or acknowledge you in any way?"

"No, the garage door opened and she drove away. Unless

she looked in her rear view mirror or back over her shoulder, I don't believe she would have seen me. That was the last time I saw her."

"Ms. Baker, there's one more question I have to ask. Was Belinda Dunstan involved with anyone?"

Ms. Baker's features clouded and she looked at her hands. "Not to my knowledge," she said carefully. "But remember there are always rumors about people of the Dunstan's status."

"Thank you, Ms. Baker. I believe that is all for now. If you think of anything later, even if it seems trivial or insignificant, please call me. My cell number is on this card. Oh, and would you please tell Ms. McCaffey we'd like to see her now."

"Yes, of course, and before you leave I'll bring the information you requested."

Earnestine McCaffey entered the sunroom. She wore a white chef's jacket over knit slacks. Although in her sixties she looked much younger and unlike some cooks her age she had managed to remain trim and fit. She had been employed by the Dunstans for nearly ten years.

"Thank you for taking the time to talk to us Ms. McCaffey. I'm Detective Maddingley and this is Detective Reardon. We want to go over the details of this past weekend. Please describe your activities Saturday and Sunday."

"As Ms. Baker probably already told you, the Dunstans gave us time off from Saturday afternoon until Sunday morning."

"What duties did you carry out Saturday?" asked Reardon.

"I prepared breakfast of course and then a light lunch

of chicken soup and sandwiches. Since the weather was so nice Mrs. Dunstan ate by the pool."

"Was she alone?"

"Yes, she said she wanted to spend the afternoon reading and getting some sun before going to that engagement party."

"Did Mrs. Dunstan consume alcohol at lunch?"

"No more than usual, maybe two or three glasses of white wine."

"Does Dr. Dunstan consume much alcohol?"

"In my experience he drinks very little and then never until the evening meal."

"What did you do after lunch?"

"I cleaned up and baked some cookies for the Doctor. He loves coconut macaroons and very thin little ginger snaps. I put them in two cookie jars that belonged to his mother. He's very sentimental. Then I left the mansion at about half past two and spent the rest of the afternoon walking my dog and reading in the park. I like romance novels. This time I ran into an old friend and we spent several hours together. I can give you his name and phone number if it's needed."

"Yes, please write it on this. Now how did you spend the rest of Saturday?"

"Charlie, my friend, came back with me and we had dinner in my quarters in the attached wing. It has a nice little kitchen back there. He left at about nine o'clock."

"Did you see the Dunstans return?" asked Maddingley.

"Yes, at about ten."

"Did you check your watch or clock?"

"I have an old mantel clock that belonged to my

grandmother. It still keeps very good time. I distinctly remember that it chimed the hour just as they came up the driveway into the courtyard. I was at the sink and the window above it looks out on the garage area."

"What did you see?"

"Dr. Dunstan drove up in that maroon English car. Mrs. Dunstan seemed to be asleep beside him. He pulled into the garage and the door closed behind them."

"Mrs. Dunstan was asleep?"

"She appeared to be, she was slumped to one side leaning against the door. I couldn't see her face since the light was rather dim inside the car."

"What else transpired that night and Sunday?"

"I went to bed at midnight and arose at around eight. I often sleep late on Sunday morning since Dr. Dunstan likes to play golf early and breakfasts at the club with friends. Mrs. Dunstan prefers to sleep late Sunday so as usual I prepared a breakfast tray and placed it on the console table beside the door to her suite at eleven. I always knock to let her know it's there."

"Did she eat breakfast?" asked Maddingley thoughtfully.

"Later I went back to pick up the tray—she usually puts it outside her door. A couple of things, toast and bacon, were gone but she didn't touch the eggs. Funny, but she didn't have any coffee either."

"Did you see Mrs. Dunstan leave?"

"It was sometime after one o'clock. I was passing the French doors that lead from the kitchen to the driveway. The garage door opened and she drove away in that little Volkswagen convertible. I noticed because it makes a rumbling sound—not too loud, but very distinct."

"Did she say or do anything and how was she dressed?"

"I remember a scarf covering her head and she was wearing sunglasses. She had on a print sundress. She didn't wave or look in my direction. I don't think she saw me."

"Did she return?"

"I haven't seen her or the car since."

"Can you think of anything else?"

"Well, I hate to say this, but when she leaves like that she probably has a hangover. Otherwise she honks and waves even if no one sees her. Please don't tell Dr. Dunstan I said that."

"I don't think that'll be necessary. If you think of anything else, no matter how insignificant it may seem, call my cell number on this card. Please tell Mrs. Kepple to come in."

Matty Kepple entered the room and stood in front of the detectives. Although heavier than Earnestine McCaffey, she still appeared fit with a pleasant grandmotherly smile.

"Please have a seat, Mrs. Kepple. I'm Peggy Reardon and this Clayton Maddingley. We're detectives with the Vestavia Hills Police Department."

"First how long have you worked for the Dunstans?"

"Oh, I believe about six years," replied Mrs. Kepple nervously as she sat down.

"You don't live on the property like Ms. Baker or Ms. McCaffey?"

"That's right, my husband and I live a few minutes away, down the mountain in Homewood. Actually both my husband and I work here. We come in three days a week—Monday, Wednesday, and Friday."

"What are your duties?"

"I do the house cleaning and laundry. Ned does the yard work. We're both semi-retired so this is a perfect job for us. I clean all the rooms except for Mrs. Dunstan's suite, Ms. Baker handles that."

"What did you do the Monday after Mrs. Dunstan disappeared?"

"As usual I gathered up all the clothes. Most I laundered here, but some things went to the drycleaners. I also dusted and vacuumed, cleaned the bathrooms, and mopped the floors. Ms. McCaffey keeps a very tidy kitchen so there was little to do in there. Ned trimmed a few boxwoods and azaleas, mulched several areas, and put in some bedding plants. He likes to mow on Wednesdays so the yard doesn't look too freshly cut on the weekend."

"What about Mrs. Dunstan's things? Did you notice anything unusual?"

"No, not really, I did take her new black cocktail dress to the dry cleaners. It seemed to be very clean but she likes her evening outfits to be cleaned after each time she wears them. The rest of her clothes I did here and gave them to Ms. Baker to put away. Oh, wait there was one peculiar thing."

"And that would be?" coaxed Maddingley.

"Her bathrobe and cocktail dress, they didn't smell like her."

"They didn't smell like her? Please explain."

"Mrs. Dunstan uses some rather distinctive bath oils and lotions. Her robe had been worn but I didn't smell anything. Her robes and other clothes are odorless after cleaning, but after use there's always the scent of those oils and lotions. They have a very pleasant odor."

15

MONA ABBINGTON HATED working at one of the hole-in-the-wall mini knockoffs of Wal-Mart that had sprouted like malignant toadstools in small towns and rural areas across the southeast. She resented the low-paying long hours and lack of benefits and struggled to keep her son and daughter clothed and fed. *I feel sorry for people comin' in here. They waste most of their money on cheap Chinese crap, candy, beer, and cigarettes.*

She became a volunteer firefighter before she divorced but only received a small stipend based upon fire calls. Her ex-husband had been recently imprisoned for manufacturing methamphetamines and what little child support he paid had disappeared years before.

Her day ended at noon and she headed south along a county road. Much of the countryside included scenic views, small farms, and neatly tended yards but in places the road was bordered by old house trailers whose yards were littered with junk lawnmowers and abandoned plastic toys. She turned onto Interstate 22 and headed east toward Birmingham. Her best friend had told her of a pawnshop in Ensley that sometimes bought things without asking questions. "Be careful," she said. "The owner's Arab."

Mona strongly distrusted Arabs since most of the rural convenience stores were owned by them. One had even tried to convince her to marry his twenty-year-old son so the boy could stay in the States. *That bastard tried to buy me for a measly two thousand dollars!*

Birmingham and the Ensley neighborhood, in particular, always frightened her. The local television news programs from Birmingham stations seemed to carry a constant litany of violent crime. *God I hope this old car doesn't break down!*

Indeed Ensley looked as bad as she expected. A few of the homes had been recently painted and some front yards appeared recently mown. But many of the houses were abandoned and with collapsing porches and roofs. On one street corner two prostitutes in miniskirts and ridiculously high clogs waved at passersby. She glanced at the little map her friend had sketched. *That place must be at the next intersection.*

Indeed at the corner of Cromwell Street and Avenue Zeta sat a small cluster of old stucco storefronts. A sign outlined in twinkling lights proclaimed "Abraham's." Closely-spaced iron bars covered its door and single window. She drove past and parked several spaces away beside a rusty ice cream truck whose tinny speakers blared incessantly. *I hate "Turkey in the Straw!" Why doesn't he shut that thing off!*

She walked up to the pawnshop's front door. There was no door knob, only a button with a note reading "ring for entry." She pushed the button and a few seconds later a metallic click announced the unlocking of the door. With some trepidation she pushed the door open and entered. It was hot and dank inside and her eyes strained to adjust to the dim light. With a click the door locked behind her. *Uh-oh.*

From the back of the store came a voice. "May I help you?"

She squinted as her eyes adjusted and she could see a bearded man seated behind a counter at the end of two rows of dusty display cases. "Ah, yes," she stammered. "I have a ring I'd like to sell but I can't give my name."

"Well, come here then," he said gesturing with his hand. "Let me see it."

She pulled the ring from her purse and handed it across the counter. The man put a jeweler's loupe to his eye and peered at it intently. He examined the inside of the setting and carefully looked at the stone from several sides. "It is real," he said quietly, "and you want to sell this for cash, no questions asked?"

She nodded.

"I give you a thousand dollars."

"It's worth much more than that—make it twenty-five hundred."

"But if no questions and I don't hold for police, I give you twelve hundred."

That payday loan's due now and those assholes are bleeding me to death. "Okay, I'll take it," she said with some resignation. *That'll be enough to pay off the balance and end the payments—at least until the next time. And there'll be enough left to buy some clothes for the kids.*

The jeweler counted out twelve one-hundred dollar bills and smiled.

16

"DR. FUENTES, LET'S go over what happened during and after the party the night before Belinda Dunstan went missing," said Detective Maddingley.

"Think carefully before answering our questions, even the smallest, seemingly trivial detail could be important," said Detective Reardon. *He's one good lookin' guy, no wonder so many gals are after him.*

"Yes ma'am."

"Okay, what time did you arrive?"

"My date and I got there about ten after seven."

"Why so exact?" asked Detective Reardon.

"I recall looking at the dashboard clock, it was just after seven. I try to be punctual. Allowing ten minutes to walk from the parking garage to the club would make the time close to ten after seven."

"Were the Dunstans already there?"

"No, they came in maybe ten minutes later."

Maddingley nodded. *That fits with the security cam recording.*

"What was Mrs. Dunstan's condition when she got there?"

"Rather subdued at first—not as talkative as usual."

"Had she been drinking?"

"I couldn't say."

"Did she drink at the party?"

"Yes."

"How much would you estimate?"

"I wasn't counting, but I don't think I ever saw her without a glass in hand."

"Did Dr. Dunstan say much of anything to her?"

"Not much that I saw, but on several occasions he did ask her to put down her drink and have something to eat."

"Did she become intoxicated?"

"Increasingly, as the evening progressed."

"Did her mood change?"

"She became more animated and vocal."

"Were you aware of any substance abuse problems?" asked Reardon.

"Until that evening only in a vague way, Dr. Dunstan once confided that she had been in rehab more than once. Then as we took her to their car he apologized for her behavior and said she'd gotten out of rehab in March."

"Did she or anyone else cause a 'scene' or disturbance?"

"In the past she sometimes made unappreciated comments about my Hispanic heritage. That night she referred to me as 'Cuban' and called me 'Little Ricky.'"

"Did she do anything else?"

"Yes, she pulled me out on the dance floor and rubbed against me in a very inappropriate manner."

"What happened then?"

"Dr. Dunstan intervened. I helped him get her to the parking deck and into their car. She could hardly walk and her speech was badly slurred. The last time I saw her was when they went down the exit ramp."

"Did you feel animosity or anger towards her?"

"Well, she could be charming when sober. I pitied her more than anything else."

"What did you do the rest of the evening?"

"We left the party at about ten o'clock and went for coffee. I dropped my girlfriend off at her condo a couple of hours later."

"We'll need to interview her as well as part of our investigative protocol."

"Sure, I'll text Beth's name, address, and phone number to you."

Maddingley mulled over Dr. Fuentes account. It dovetailed nicely with the security video from the parking deck. *We're gonna need more to go on. But we still hafta review the video from the Dunstan's security system.*

Detective Reardon connected an external hard drive to her office computer. *Wow, thirty-two days of high definition video—impressive!*

She initiated a program that scanned the terabytes of data for movement and watched in amazement. *Funny how hours can pass between people coming and going, but this program makes it appear that courtyard's a busy place. And the programmer was thoughtful enough to have the time cue read in a.m. and p.m.—I hate twenty-four hour clocks!*

Indeed, only minutes passed as days went by on the screen. Dr. Dunstan left early each morning, while his wife often drove away around noon or early afternoon. The cook, Mrs. Dunstan's personal assistant, cleaning lady, and groundskeeper appeared driving or walking across the screen. Each night a curious raccoon included the courtyard in his rounds. A month passed and the activities of each day of the week became apparent. The comings and goings fit a predictable pattern and confirmed what they had been told.

The video approached seven o'clock, Saturday evening, the fourteenth. One of the garage doors opened and the Dunstans, dressed in evening attire, left in the Bristol. In seconds the time cue on the upper right of the monitor jumped to 8:55. A man earlier identified as Mrs. McCaffey's friend Charlie left in what appeared to be a Honda Accord. Amelia Baker returned—9:56. The cue moved to 10:02, the Dunstans returned. Belinda Dunstan lay slumped against the passenger side door. *Asleep or unconscious? So far this fits with the interviews about that night*, Reardon thought as the garage door closed. The raccoon crossed the screen. *There goes Bandit.*

Almost instantly Dunstan left in his Mercedes—six o'clock Sunday morning. Amelia Baker left, 9:45, then returned, 11:15. The time cue jumped to 1:11—early Sunday afternoon. A different garage door opened and a Volkswagen Karmann Ghia convertible backed out, turned around, and left. Belinda Dunstan wearing a sundress, headscarf, and sunglasses sat behind the wheel. Another jump and the doctor returned, presumably from his two rounds of golf.

Reardon watched as the images advanced through Monday and Tuesday. The same weekday patterns repeated—except there was no Belinda Dunstan. *All the statements we took appear to agree. But where is she?*

"Got a minute?" asked Chief Haskell standing in the doorway.

"Sure, come on in," said Maddingley. "What's up?"

"Look we all hate political interference, but it's this Dunstan thing." The detectives stared steely-eyed at Haskell. "A couple of the councilmembers approached me. They're very concerned about Belinda Dunstan's disappearance. Any leads so far?"

"At this point we haven't eliminated any possibilities— accident, carjacking, kidnapping, medical problem, whatever," said Reardon.

"I know there are ongoing cases, but we need to concentrate on this one."

"Well, patrol has checked out the routes she may have taken after she drove away on Sunday. Cops from everywhere around and the sheriffs' departments of Jefferson and neighboring counties have nothing to report. The Troopers reported no accidents that might be relevant. This morning we called every hospital and morgue in a hundred miles. Reardon and I are going to drive west on Shades Crest all the way down through Shelby County and then to Bibb County since she liked to drive that way sometimes. We're going to stop at businesses and show photos of her and her car. Maybe someone will remember her."

"That sounds like a good approach. Make some more copies of those photos and Jenkins and I will go east on Shades Crest and then down 280. I've got a few calls to make, so why don't we leave in about forty-five minutes."

"I'll get the copies to you shortly," said Maddingley.

"Clayton, while you're doing that, I wanna look at this video again."

She backed up to Saturday and played the recording again—this time in slow motion. Yet nothing appeared suspicious or out of place. Again she reviewed the recording, this time even slower. And then when early Sunday afternoon was reached, she saw it.

She slowed the video even further as the garage door opened and the convertible backed out into the early afternoon sunlight. A quick glint emanated from the point that the driver's left hand gripped the steering wheel. *What's that?*

"Hey Clayton, take a look at this." She backed the video to Friday and went through the weekend as he peered over her shoulder.

"Watch carefully as her car moves out of the garage," Reardon said as she slowed the video. The car eased out of the garage and into the sunshine. Something flashed from the area of the steering wheel.

"Can you zoom in on that area?" The screen filled with an image that framed the upper driver side door and part of the windshield. The driver's left hand could be seen at the ten o'clock position on the steering wheel. As she slowly turned the wheel a quick gleam sparkled in the sunlight.

"See that?" muttered Reardon almost to herself as she froze the frame and zoomed even closer.

"That's a huge diamond ring," exclaimed Maddingley, "one of the biggest I've ever seen!"

"And her assistant told us she never wore pieces like that when she dressed informally! Is there a ring like that on the inventory Amelia Baker gave us?"

"Hmmm, let's see," said Reardon as she pulled a page from the case file and scanned the list for a few moments. "It doesn't look like any of the diamond rings on here fits the description of that thing. What is going on?"

"This is getting 'curiouser and curiouser.'"

"Clayton, look at this area I isolated on her upper neck, kinda behind her ear, and partially covered by the scarf. Is that a tattoo or bruise?" He magnified the frame even further. "The image is starting to get fuzzy, but it looks like part of a tattooed name. I believe I'm seeing 'Ki.'"

"Before the Chief came in I was going through the Facebook photos from the engagement party. Belinda Dunstan shows up in a couple of them."

Typically for such an occasion, the first photo showed the Dunstans with several other couples toasting the camera with their cocktails. "Can't see behind her ear in that one. Here's the other shot." Belinda Dunstan appeared on the right side of the photo, glass in hand, engaged in animated conversation with another reveler. Her hairstyle revealed her neck and exposed the area behind her ear.

"She's got on those earrings Baker mentioned, her hair's pulled back, and there's nothing else showing on her neck 'cept for those pearls and there's definitely nothing behind her ear. And I don't see that big diamond ring either."

"How very interesting," Reardon mused, "think they had time to stop at a tattoo parlor on the way home? And what about that big ring?"

"That gal in the car *ain't* Belinda Dunstan!"

"We've got to get more evidence or a body. Then, the good doctor has some explaining to do."

17

IT WAS A glorious spring day. Dalton and Genn finished their morning lectures with enough time to drive down to Big Tom County for lunch at one of the area's venerable institutions—Hastings' Fish Camp. Owned by Genn's cousins, Hastings' had been in business for nearly a century in a hewn-timber building that had stood for almost two hundred years overlooking the Tombigbee River.

"I love Tuscaloosa, but whenever we drive through this countryside, I'm sure my blood pressure drops ten points."

"Lose twenty pounds and we won't hafta drive down here just for the health benefits."

He reached for her hand. "Aww Genn, you know I'm workin' on it!"

"Yeah right—then start running with me in the mornings."

"Sweetie, you know I'm not a mornin' person."

"Ha! Then why do you get so amorous at five o'clock?" she said pushing his hand away.

Immediately south of Whitby modest homes lined the highway. "Remember when that old sharecropper shack burned down? The way the chimney stood there for years

113

and then somebody built a little house around it. And look at those two red rocking chairs on the porch—they gotta be Bama fans!"

"Dalton, give me a break, you've told me that umpteenth times!"

"Sorry, but it's such a good story and a great example of recycling."

"I know, I know!" said Genn rolling her eyes.

Around them the Black Belt Prairie rolled to the horizon in all directions and the gray pavement of Highway 95 lay before them like a ribbon across the countryside. The road disappeared in the trees atop a line of low hills stretching across the county and marking the southern boundary of the prairie.

"Tell me again—what's that ridge called?" asked Genn. "I keep forgetting."

"That's the Ripley Cuesta, better known as the Chunnenuggee Hills. It means 'long high ridge' in Choctaw. We made a couple of field trips along that steep north slope back in one of my geology courses. Some of those fossils you found came from an exposed section of the Ripley on that high riverbank."

"I would love to time travel and see what this area looked like all those millions of years ago."

"There were lotsa big hungry critters back then. You might get a quick look around before some reptile invited you to lunch," he said clacking his teeth together.

"I've been invited to lunch by 'reptiles' before. But not like any of those."

As they approached the intersection of Highways 95 and 12 at Coleman's Corner, the scattered cedars and Osage oranges became mixed with pine and hackberry trees. Possumhaw bushes and potato vines grew in the roadside fences. All that remained of the little crossroads community were a few battered mobile homes, the collapsed ruins of a house and a country store engulfed by a blanket of kudzu, and the abandoned elementary school.

They turned right on Highway 12 towards the Tombigbee River. About half a mile down the road they approached Coleman's Corner United Methodist Church.

"You wanna stop?"

"Not today. I get too sad. We'll be here for the next Homecoming. Mama always knew how much I loved her, she was only fifty-five," said Genn, her eyes downcast and her voice breaking.

Wilhelmina, "Willie," Hastings lay in the church cemetery with seven generations of both sides of Genn's family all the way back to Zachariah Hastings, who came from South Carolina and fought in the War of 1812 and the bloody Alabama Indian Wars against the Creeks. In the 1830s, President Andrew Jackson issued a land grant to old Zach for his military service. Over the decades after his death, his heirs divided the land and sold most of it. Genn grew up on the only remaining portion.

"Don't ever forget, I want to be beside her with you on my left. Now let's talk of happier things."

Dalton reached over and gently held her hand. "Whatcha gonna have for lunch?"

Laughing, she pushed his hand away. "Do you ever stop thinking about food?"

He smiled. *Only when I'm thinking about sex.*

As they neared the river, the land dropped away while

the road stayed above the floodplain. Intermittent and mysterious stands of cypress and boggy patches covered with cattails and mallow mingled with the cedars, pines, and hackberries. Just before reaching the river bridge they turned off and drove through the entrance gate to the restaurant. Cotton and soybean fields lined the mile long drive.

Lowrene Latham, the long-time manager, opened the door with a smile and led them to a window table with a panoramic view of the river. "Miss Genevieve, what'll you have?"

"Blackened catfish sounds good. Add a tossed salad with vinaigrette dressing and a plain baked potato."

"How about you 'fessor?"

"Lowrene, I'm gonna be bad today. I'll have the fried catfish with fries and that mayonnaise based coleslaw—oh, and extra hushpuppies."

"Dalton J. Randolph!" Lowrene smiled. "Honey, when I'm gonna be 'bad' I go find me a good-lookin' man. To hell with food!" Genn could barely keep water from shooting out her nose.

"Never mind, I guess I'll have the same as her," said Dalton, resolved to his diet.

"And no dessert for this big hungry critter," Genn chimed in with a smile. "But I still might make him run behind the Tahoe back up to the highway."

While waiting for their meal a towboat pushed six barges into view. "I've always wanted to make the downstream trip to Mobile on one of those," said Dalton.

"Thinking of changing careers?"

"Naw, just daydreaming, besides it would be great to see all the scenery and I've always heard they have great food."

"Well, here's some great food," said Genn as Lowrene brought in their orders.

As they ate two groups of diners came in and sat near them. All were acquaintances or cousins and pleasant conversation and laughter filled the dining room.

After a half-hour in the rocking chairs on the Fish Camp's creaky front porch, Dalton rose and stretched. "Time to head to Tuscaloosa I guess. It'll be a nice drive, especially with all the flowers in bloom."

—∽∽—

Crows cawed in the distance as afternoon sunlight streamed through the dirty windows of the trailer. Edgar had arisen just before dawn to check for a delivery and then lay back down and slept late. The boss had closed the shop for a couple of days to have two new heavy-duty truck lifts installed.

I hate waking up with a dry mouth. He swung to the side of the filthy mattress, his hand fumbling along the floor reaching for a water bottle. He stumbled to his feet and the coughing began instantly. "Where's that *damned* water?" he uttered. Kicking dirty clothes aside he stepped over to a tiny refrigerator. It quit working weeks earlier, but he didn't care. It was still a good place to keep a few bottles of water or cans of beer. He washed out his mouth and drank the rest. *I'll get sumthin later, maybe at that gas station in Whitby. But this time of day their little deli won't have none of them biscuits with fried baloney. Gotta clean up, but first I need a smoke.* He lit a cigarette and inhaled deeply.

Edgar went outside, stripped off, and doused himself with water from a plastic jug. The water felt chilly and he shivered. Bad hygiene was one of the signs of drug use and his parole officer would notice. *I'm not a stupid junkie. I've kept away from that shit.* His friends in prison were right. *Stay clean, stay outta trouble, keep a low profile, and get out early. That was the motto and it worked.* He lathered up a little and rinsed off before putting on jeans and a tee shirt. *Gotta look presentable.* He looked in a broken piece of mirror attached to the side of the trailer. No longer clean shaven, he sported a closely-cropped beard. He reminded himself that he needed to clean up the trailer. *Well, at least get rid of the fast food bags, beer cans, and cigarette butts.*

—⁀ⁱⁱⁱ—

From Coleman's Corner, Highway 95 was the shortest way home. "Let's stop for a moment," said Dalton as they approached Saint-Cyr. He pulled off the road at the same spot where he'd taken the rainbow and browse line photos. "It sure looks different on a sunny day."

"And especially with all those little yellow flowers," mused Genn.

Dalton inspected the heavy padlock and chain on the gate. "I'll bet there's a hidden key,"

"That's none of our business, let's get going."

He reached around the gate post and lightly slid his fingers along the backside, careful to avoid anything sharp. There were no nails or splinters, just a smoothly-weathered surface. As he reached further down almost to the ground his little finger brushed against a thin piece of wire. *That's odd*, he thought as he gently tugged at it. Something slipped into his hand.

"I'll be danged, look at this!" He held up a short piece of thin rusty wire and jiggled the key dangling from it.

"This was pushed into a hole almost at the bottom of the fence post, any lower and I'd have stuck my hand in that fire ant bed."

"Put that back! We aren't opening that gate—no way!" exclaimed Genn. "Let's just go home and forget about this, you've obsessed enough."

"That's a gravel drive so there'll be no tire tracks, plus I'll bet Edgar's not here. Lucius said he has a job over in Mississippi near his parole officer's office so he can be checked on. That's across the river and the next county plus it's a work day."

"Dalton, don't be a fool! He could show up at any moment!"

"It won't take ten minutes to walk over past those trees and take a quick look. We could always claim the gate was open and we didn't want the cows to get out on the highway."

"Yeah right, then if that's so, why didn't we just close the gate and go on our way? An open gate out here's not an invitation to go in. This property's posted! Can't you see those signs on the fence posts?" exclaimed Genn angrily pointing. "The last thing we want to do is get caught trespassing on that creep's property. Let's go!"

"Well, IF we got caught we could claim we wanted to see Edgar with the hope that he had changed and that we wanted to let 'bygones be bygones' about things that happened years ago."

"Dalton, that's not gonna fly. He hasn't changed ... he's only worse. Remember Edgar killed a man at that honky-tonk over on the state line. If not for that slick lawyer, he'd still be on Parchman Farm over in the Mississippi Delta. God only knows what he picked up in that place!"

"I know what will work! We can claim the truck broke down and since there's such poor cell coverage out here we walked in hoping he might have a landline phone. We don't need the key, I'm putting it back."

He opened the hood of their Tahoe and climbed over the gate.

"Dalton this is crazy!" she screamed following him.

18

EDGAR'S UNCLE'S 1968 Ford F150 pickup sat in front of the trailer. Years of hard use left it with dents, faded blue paint, and rust. The bed was so riddled with holes that once when he tried to haul sand, little dunes formed whenever he stopped. A weathered sheet of plywood solved that problem. He did just enough mechanically to keep her running. However, at considerable expense, he had outfitted her with a set of mud tires especially designed for the local gumbo. One of the mechanics he helped in Meridian always teased him, but actually wanted to buy the truck as a restoration project for his annoying teenage daughter who hung around the shop, constantly asking questions.

"Man that thang would be sweet with a new Cummins diesel, disc brakes, heavy-duty suspension, bed, and electrical system. Just stabilize the rust and she'd be one bad-ass lookin' ride! I might even keep it for myself after 'Bitsy' does all the work. I'm proud of that little gal. She's a chip off this old block."

Edgar always declined the offers with a slight smile. *I'd hafta get a new ride and that would cost more than I'm willing to pay. Maybe I'll do that work myself one of these days.*

The flowers in the pasture surrounded them. "It's beautiful out here," he said as they approached the trees lining the stream. "The cattle must've been moved to another pasture so our browse line is starting to grow out. I'll bet those weren't Edgar's cattle, he probably leased the grazing rights to the people next door."

"We don't have time to enjoy the view, Dalton," said Genn furiously through clenched teeth. "Check out what you wanted to see and let's get outta here!"

They passed through the narrow line of trees and across the little stream. "The body must've been about here, but I don't see anything, just dirt and grass. Let's go a little further."

"Are you insane?"

"It's just a little ways, come on!"

The road sloped up to a high spot overlooking the property. A few bodock trees exhibited luxuriant foliage and there were several ancient cedars with weathered gray bark. It appeared likely that this had been the site of Saint-Cyr. A tangled mass of rusty barbed wire and rotten fence posts lay rolled up next to a large tree. Three strands were still attached and cut off ends of wire protruded from the other side of the trunk. Close by lay a large sheet of rusty corrugated roofing.

"This looks suspicious. Somebody's moved that tin and there're a couple of cigarette butts beside it." He grasped a corner, careful not to get cut, and dragged the tin aside uncovering a hole about two feet in diameter.

"What's this?" asked Dalton as he peered inside. "Animals don't dig burrows this wide and certainly not into chalk. This is manmade and smells *horrible!*"

"Just cover that back up and let's get outta here, now. Did you hear me Dalton? NOW!" she yelled.

"All right, let's get back to the highway." Dalton shoved the tin back over the hole.

Edgar got in and fired up the truck. The cab was hot and reeked from decades of leaking oil and transmission fluid, cigarettes, and mildewed upholstery. Years ago his uncle replaced a broken window crank handle with an old rusty pair of Vice-Grip pliers. *Clumsy, but it does the job.*

He flicked a cigarette butt out the window and exhaled. The old truck started and the gears ground as he shifted into low and pulled away with a jerk. *Damn clutch needs work too.* As he topped the rise two wide-eyed people standing beside the road turned to stare.

What the hell are they doin' here?

The sound of a vehicle reached their ears. Trailing blue smoke, a battered old truck came over the rise from the backside of the property. It approached Genn and Dalton and stopped. *Nowhere to run or hide,* thought Dalton.

"What are y'all doin' here?" demanded Edgar. "This is private property with a locked gate! Didn't you see them signs? Can't you read?"

"I'm sorry," said Dalton. "Our truck broke down and we couldn't get cell coverage long enough to make a call, it just winks on and off. We thought someone must live down this road since there's a mail box by the gate. We're hoping you've got a landline and we can call for help. There's not much traffic on the highway and no one would stop."

"Well, you're just shit outta luck! Do you geniuses see

any phone lines running across this pasture or buried cable signs? And it's a waste of money to have a cell phone out here. Most of the time there's no bars."

"I guess I just didn't think about that."

"Mister, we're really sorry," said Genn grabbing Dalton's arm and turning to leave. "We'll go right back to our truck and I'm sure someone will stop after a while."

"Wait a minute! Don't I know you two? You're that nerd kid from high school in Whitby and you're his skinny-ass girlfriend. Do you remember who I am?"

Edgar glanced over at the rusty sheet of tin roofing. "Why the hell've you been screwin' around with that?" Edgar pulled a pistol from beneath the seat and got out of the truck.

"We didn't do that, honest. Look, there's no need to be angry, please stay calm, we're leaving right now," said Genn still pulling at Dalton's arm.

"You ain't talkin' your way outta this and you ain't leaving my property. Move that piece of tin and get down in that damn hole, now!"

"You can't be serious, there's no way to climb down and it's too deep to jump into!"

"And you claimed you didn't know it was there? Empty your pockets on the ground and drop everything. Tie this rope to that bodock and lower yourself. I know both of you can do it. I remember seeing you climb ropes in high school gym class. If you could climb up that one, then you can *damn* well climb down this one!"

"But that one had knots, this one's nylon and we'll burn our hands," said Dalton.

"Please let us leave," said Genn approaching Edgar.

Her plea was met with a backhanded slap to her mouth that knocked her to the ground and flung her glasses to one side.

Dalton started towards him but Edgar chambered a round, extended his arm, and stuck the pistol in Dalton's face. "Shut up and get down that hole! Do it NOW!"

"I'll go first," interjected Genn rising from all fours and grabbing her glasses. Thorns tore at her as she wrapped the rope around the tree. Now her lip and arms were bleeding. "Just please, please don't hurt him," she pleaded.

Genn grasped the rope and backed into the hole, the stench overwhelming her. She gagged as her head disappeared below the rim.

"You next *smart* boy."

Dalton grasped the rope and began descending. It had been years since he had done anything like this. His arms ached and the rope burned his hands—a painful reminder of the weight he had gained over the years. Reaching the bottom, he could hear Genn vomiting.

"You okay?" he asked taking her into his arms.

"No, I'm not!" she screamed. "Your pig-headed obsession got us into this!"

"But you're bleeding!"

"Those are just scratches, but the smell and all that dust made me puke. Why did you have to go over that gate? We might die down here!"

"Heads up, here's your wallet and cell phone! Good luck gettin' any coverage," laughed Edgar as he pulled up the rope.

The only light came through the small opening above. But before their eyes could adjust to the darkness, Edgar

125

slid the piece of tin back over the hole. They could hear him start the pickup and drive away.

"That sorry-ass bastard is smarter than I thought," said Dalton. "He doesn't want to chance my phone or wallet being found and he knows we can't call from down here. I wonder what he'll do with the Tahoe."

"And I left my phone and purse in the truck … that was stupid. But not as stupid as you dragging us out here!"

Dalton activated his phone, no reception bars came up but the screen faintly illuminated their surroundings. They were inside an enlarged chamber beneath the entrance hole. *This must be the cistern shown on the building survey drawings and photos. The little gazebo up top might have burned when the big house went up in the forties or rotted down.*

As best as he could estimate, the cistern spanned nearly twenty feet and reached upwards at least fifteen or sixteen feet to the entrance shaft that extended about six feet more to the surface. He did a quick mental calculation.

"Wow, this old cistern can hold almost thirty thousand gallons of water and look at those pick marks on the walls. Can you imagine slaves working down here chipping away at that chalk?"

"If you're gonna be an *engineer* all the time," said Genn sarcastically. "Why don't you *engineer* a way out of this mess you got us into?"

Directly beneath the opening lay a lumpy pile covered in white dust. They had landed on it as they descended. Genn stared in disbelief at the pile.

"Oh my God! Oh my God! Those are bodies! We were standing on bodies!"

"Damn ... those are bodies," whispered Dalton as Genn clung to him shivering.

"We can't stay down here, we've got to get out," she cried, panic rising in her voice.

Dalton could hear his heart pounding. *What have I gotten us into? We may die down here!*

"I can't handle this," sobbed Genn. She turned and began walking along the wall, her hands feverishly feeling for a way out.

"We've got to calm down," he said pulling her back towards him. "We've got to think logically, panic won't get us out."

They stood embracing for nearly half an hour, Genn's body shook as she sobbed. "Why Dalton, why," she said repeatedly.

By now their eyes had adjusted to the darkness. The dusty pile of corpses seemed to glow eerily in the low light. "Look, there's a woman in a cocktail dress on top, she hasn't been down here long. And why aren't there flies everywhere?"

"Remember that empty bag we walked by near the gate? It said 'Hydrated Lime' in big letters. That's actually calcium hydroxide. Sometimes it's used by farmers when soil is too acidic. But that's not a problem in this area. I wondered about that. He's been dumping it in the hole to keep down the flies and speed up decomposition. I talk about calcium hydroxide in my water treatment classes since it's used to adjust the pH of water so pipes won't corrode."

"It might help with the flies, but it's not doing much for the odor!"

"The body in the photo must be one of these corpses. That's what Edgar's up to! Someone must be paying him to dispose of bodies. They couldn't be from around here or we'd hear about lotsa missing people. Some of them have been down here for quite some time." Indeed some of the bodies were little more than disarticulated skeletons.

"Leave the sleuthing to Lucius! Now how do we get out? Those slaves must've used a ladder or steps."

Dalton scanned the walls and floor but nothing like a ladder could be seen. "It must've been pulled out or rotted away and there aren't any obvious steps or handholds either. Think you could climb up? I've seen you on that wall at the rec center."

"I don't see any places to grip or push against. But we gotta try. Gimme a boost ... but first turn off your cellphone. Don't run the battery down."

The darkness was almost complete except under the opening at the top. A faint glow filtered around the edges of the tin and one slender ray of sunlight projected through a nail hole.

"Here Genn," Dalton said as he stood against the chalk wall with his hands cupped. "Step up and stand on my shoulders, I'll brace the back of your legs."

Genn nimbly climbed over her husband and stood erect against the wall. "Move out just a few inches so I can lean forward slightly. That's it, this is more stable." She could feel pick marks almost two centuries old as she ran her hands over the rough surface.

"Shift a little to your right. Some of these indentations are almost deep enough to get a grip." Her mouth ached terribly and she could feel a scab starting to form on her lower lip.

"Stand still, don't shift your weight, I'm going to push up and see if I can grab what I think is a little ledge just outta reach. I think I feel the edge of it."

For a moment Genn dug her fingers into the little ledge. But she couldn't support her weight enough to pull up. Her left foot slipped off Dalton's shoulder and she slid down into his arms. His reaction broke her fall, but they both stumbled off the pile of corpses and fell in an embrace on the cistern floor.

"You okay?" he whispered as he brushed the dust from her face. "Let's don't try that again, I'm afraid you'll get hurt."

"There's no other way. We either get out or we die slowly down here. That lime dust is beginning to make my throat and eyes burn. Maybe I could hold on to those pick marks if they could be dug out some more. That chalk's soft, but what could we use?"

"Yeah, like those foot holes the Acoma Indians from the old days dug out on the side of that mesa in New Mexico! Remember we saw that on our trip. But that bastard took our keys, maybe there're some old nails or scrap iron down here. We can't use the cell phone for light since that'll run down the battery. Why don't we move along the floor and see if we can feel anything with our feet and hands?"

They carefully shuffled along the perimeter gently patting the floor of the cistern, encountering a few broken bricks, twigs, and pieces of rotten wood that had fallen through the opening above.

Genn felt something soft and bumpy—the thing moved. She screamed loudly, recoiling in horror. "What was that?"

The toad hopped away. "He must have fallen in," said Dalton.

"Yeah and now he's trapped like us."

"We need to be very careful; there may be snakes down here too."

"I didn't need to hear that!"

19

SHADIYAH IBRAHIM APPROACHED security screening at the Birmingham Airport with her purse and a small carry-on bag. "On the conveyor," said the TSA agent robotically.

Shadiyah complied. "Step through the gate," droned the guard. An alarm sounded.

"Stop!" ordered the guard on the other side. "Stand here."

The guard scanned the young woman's body with a hand-held wand. It detected something low on the right side of her chest. The officer gestured and immediately two female officers approached. "Come with us," one said, "through that door."

Inside the room they told Shadiyah to disrobe. "You singled me out because of my hijab!" she shouted.

"No ma'am! We did not! Ladies in hijabs come through here every day. Something on your person is setting off the alarm." The officer said as she demonstrated again with the detector wand.

"It appears something in your bra is metallic."

"Haven't you ever heard of an underwire?" asked Shadiyah sarcastically, her dark eyes flashing.

"Underwired on only one side? I don't think so. You'll hafta remove it."

"You're harassing me because I am Muslim!"

"Step behind that screen, take it off, and hand it over to Officer Bennington."

Shadiyah reluctantly complied. Officer Bennington examined the bra and pulled two sewn packets from the insert pockets. The wand sounded when passed over one of the packets.

"Ma'am, what's in here?" asked Bennington.

"It's just my engagement ring."

"There's a lot more than that in there. You'll hafta remain with us until everything is examined," said the other officer as she studied Shadiyah's Pakistani passport.

On a well-lit table under a video camera, Bennington cut the stitches sealing the packets. The right side packet contained a stack of hundred-dollar bills. The other contained a similar stack of bills and an object wrapped in gauze. *What's this? It's heavy to be so small. No wonder it set off the alarms.*

She carefully peeled away the gauze revealing a stunning ring with more fire that Bennington had ever seen. "Wow!" she whispered to her companion as she rotated the ring between her fingers. Normally cash and jewelry taken out of the country weren't considered contraband, but such elaborate concealment and cash amounting to twenty thousand dollars set off flashing red lights of suspicion.

"What do you make of this, Secilia?"

Officer Secilia Watson examined the ring with a jeweler's loupe. "Wow, 'HW' and '18k' hallmarks!" she exclaimed. "This thing's a Harry Winston—eighteen-carat white gold with a diamond of at least four carats. There's an ID number etched on the stone's girdle. Let's see if it's listed in the database."

She entered the number and almost instantly a listing appeared, "Registrant: Belinda Dunstan—Contacts: Chubb Masterpiece Insurance and Police Department, Vestavia Hills, AL."

Officer Watson made a brief call and within minutes two uniformed officers appeared.

"Ms. Ibrahim," one of the officers declared, "you are under arrest for possession of stolen property. You have the right to remain silent. Anything you say …."

"Ms. Ibrahim, tell us about this ring," said Detective Reardon pointing to a photograph.

"It's my engagement ring."

"So your fiancé gave you this ring." stated Maddingley. "Who is he?"

"My cousin in Pakistan. My parents and brother arranged the marriage."

"So he sent you this ring?"

"Yes."

"This ring is registered to a missing person from Vestavia Hills. The insurer has no record of ownership transfer. It's just not plausible for it to have been sent from here to Pakistan and back," said Reardon. Shadiyah stared at the table top in silence.

"Here's the situation," said Maddingley. "This ring was apparently stolen and may be connected to a homicide. It was in your possession and you were attempting to leave the country. How do you think a jury will react to that? At a minimum you may face several years in prison and then be deported or you could spend the rest of your life locked away."

"It's also possible you are merely in possession of stolen property—a relatively minor offence," said Reardon. "If you cooperate you may receive a few months in jail or even be on probation. Tell us the truth, that's all we want. Where did you get this ring and why were you taking it out of the country?"

Shadiyah continued to stare at the tabletop.

"Listen to me Shadiyah, a woman is missing and possibly dead. You had her ring. Tell us the truth," said Maddingley.

Shadiyah began to shake and tears welled in her eyes. "I was taking it to Abu Dhabi to sell. The money I was carrying and what the ring would have brought was to be my dowry."

"And you're marrying your cousin?" asked Reardon. "But where did you get this ring?"

"My brother owns a pawnshop. He bought it from someone who did not know its worth."

"We need your brother's name and the location of his shop."

"Cyd … Cyd Ibrahim. His shop is called Abraham's."

"And where is it located?" asked Maddingley.

"On Cromwell Street, in Ensley."

Shadiyah put her head on the table and wept.

"Mr. Ibrahim where did you get this ring?" asked Detective Maddingley.

"Think carefully before you answer," interjected Detective Reardon. "This ring relates to the search for a missing person and a possible homicide. If you purchased this ring not knowing its history you may only face a misdemeanor charge for not holding it for the required time. If you cooperate, we'll ask the authorities in your area to consider not prosecuting. Otherwise you'll be imprisoned for receiving stolen merchandise and will be deported along with forfeiting the cash your sister concealed in her clothing."

Ibrahim paused for a moment. "Okay, I will tell you what I know. A woman brought in that ring wanting to sell it 'no questions asked.' Since its value is high, greed clouded my judgment. I gave her twelve hundred dollars for it."

"Who was she?" asked Reardon.

"I do not know."

"What did she look like?" asked Maddingley.

"Young, maybe thirty years old, dark hair."

"What was she driving?"

"She must've parked around the corner. I didn't see a car."

"How was she dressed?"

"She wore tight blue jeans and a T-shirt. I would never allow my sister to wear such immodest clothing!"

"Was there anything in particular you remember about her, perhaps a tattoo?" asked Reardon.

"No tattoos that I noticed, but her T-shirt was dark blue with some sort of Christian cross. It looked like the petals of a flower. I know little of such things."

"Could you draw it?" asked Maddingley handing him a pencil and piece of paper.

Ibrahim frowned and shrugged. He picked up the pencil and began drawing.

Reardon glanced at Maddingley. "Excuse us a moment, Mr. Ibrahim."

The detectives left the room. "I know that symbol—the

cross of Saint Florian, the patron saint of firefighters," said Reardon. "My father was a fireman and wore a lapel pin in that shape, plus the trucks in his department had it painted on the doors. Now we're gettin' somewhere!"

20

AMELIA BAKER SAT nervously in an interview room at the Vestavia Hills Police Department. Down the hall in a separate room Daniel Dunstan paced impatiently.

"Ms. Baker, we have two concerns to discuss with you today," said Maddingley as he handed her a photograph.

"Do you recognize this ring?" asked Reardon.

Amelia Baker sat in stunned silence staring at the photo.

"It's registered and insured in Belinda Dunstan's name and it's not included in the inventory you gave us the other day."

"Where did you get this photo?"

"We'll discuss that later. But for now, why wasn't it included in the inventory that you gave us?"

Biting her lower lip she stared at the desk top. "I ... I don't know what to say."

"It's very important that you be truthful."

"I was frightened when you asked for a copy of the inventory. I updated it Monday morning and discovered the ring was missing and panicked."

"Why did you panic?" asked Reardon.

"I'm responsible for keeping track of Mrs. Dunstan's

jewelry. I was afraid I would lose my job and place to live. When you asked for a copy, I pulled up the spreadsheet and deleted the ring. I then printed you a new copy. I felt really, really bad about doing that and admitted to Dr. Dunstan what I had done. He told me not to worry but that it might be something important concerning Mrs. Dunstan's disappearance. He was going to call, but you called first."

"Tell us about this ring."

"It's very special—actually it's Belinda's engagement ring. When she and the Doctor got engaged, he was a medical student of limited means and could only afford something very modest. Years later after the Doctor's practice became established and he made some good investments, he purchased what he called a 'proper engagement ring.' It's a very high quality four-carat 'pillow' shape diamond surrounded by sixteen smaller stones. It's insured for replacement cost—about thirty thousand dollars. I'm the one who actually bid on that ring at auction. I was still with Mendelssohn's at the time and he asked me to buy it as a surprise for his wife."

"Why try to conceal that it was missing?"

"I was hoping it was merely mislaid or dropped somewhere around the house. I've been searching everywhere. I was afraid that if the doctor found out he would fire me! Or that people would think I took it. But I went ahead and told him. Anyway she rarely wears it."

"And why is that?"

"She only wears that ring on special occasions with family or close friends. She isn't comfortable wearing it around strangers. That's why she didn't wear it to the engagement party."

"Ms. Baker that leads to our second concern" said Maddingley. "If she so seldom wears that ring and never in public, then why did she wear it when she went for that drive Sunday afternoon, the last time she was seen?"

"I haven't the faintest idea. But what makes you think she wore it?"

"It's visible on the security video supplied by Dr. Dunstan," stated Maddingley.

"The sunlight reflected off it when Mrs. Dunstan drove away," added Reardon. "We zoomed in and it's clearly visible."

"I don't know … I don't know why she would have worn it. Where did you find it?"

"We can't say since the investigation is ongoing," said Reardon.

"Have you found her?"

"No," said Maddingley shaking his head.

"Do you think she's still alive?"

"All we can say is that the investigation continues," replied Reardon.

Maddingley cocked his head to one side. "Are you still sure you have no idea why she wore that ring?"

"No Detective, I don't."

Remember Dan, talk of her in the present tense, avoid past tense, act like she's still alive and you really care, be careful, husbands are suspected first, they'll judge you on every word, think before speaking, don't talk too much like you did before, take a deep breath, relax, don't forget, Belinda first, act concerned ….

"Good morning Dr. Dunstan," said Maddingley as he

and Reardon entered the room. "Thanks for coming in on such short notice."

"No problem, I hope you have some information about Belinda."

"Well, something has come up and we need to talk," said Maddingley as he handed a photo to Dunstan. "Recognize this ring?"

"That's Belinda's engagement ring! We call it that even though we'd been married for eleven years before I could afford it. Where did you find it?"

"That's the curious part. TSA personnel seized it at the Birmingham Airport, along with a large amount of cash. It was being smuggled out of the country by a young Pakistani woman. They found the identification number inscribed on the edge of the diamond and traced it to your wife. Do you have any idea how it came to be in that woman's possession?"

"All I know is that Amelia discovered it was missing when she inventoried Belinda's jewelry. She was terrified that I would fire her and she'd have to move out. She told me it was missing and I planned to contact you, but you called us before I could."

"Ms. Baker told us your wife didn't wear that ring to the engagement party," said Detective Reardon.

"She only wears it on special occasions around family or friends."

"Why is that?"

"She has a sort of a phobia about her fingers. Years ago she read about a thief cutting off a woman's fingers because she couldn't get her rings off. We go to a lot of events where we don't know everyone. Belinda gets nervous wearing expensive rings around strangers. For the same reason she doesn't wear it during day-to-day activities."

"It didn't bother her to wear those expensive pearls to the party."

"I guess she thinks that if she's robbed, a necklace will come off quickly. Sometimes rings are hard to remove—you know fingers sometimes swell up."

"What about her other jewelry—does she wear her expensive pieces frequently?"

"Only to social events when appropriate and certainly not during everyday activities, she thinks it's gauche."

"Dr. Dunstan, we've carefully reviewed video from your security system and when your wife left in her convertible on Sunday afternoon, she wore this ring. It's clearly visible," said Maddingley. "Why do you think she did that?"

"Really? She had it on? I have no idea."

"And you still have no idea where she went?" asked Reardon.

"No idea at all. Like I said before, she just needs to get away sometimes. But how did this Pakistani woman get hold of her ring?"

"That's still under investigation," said Maddingley. "However, I can tell you that her brother is a jeweler and pawnbroker in Birmingham. They were trying to get it to the jewelry market in Abu Dhabi where it could be sold for a large profit."

"Did they have anything to do with her disappearance?"

"Well, that's part of the investigation. But so far the pawnbroker and his sister seem to be cooperative."

"I hope this will help us find her. In the meantime, I'll

have Amelia put the ring back with Belinda's things and I'll notify the insurer it's been found."

"You can notify the insurer, but it's evidence in a missing person case. There may be local and federal actions against the pawnbroker and his sister. It has to remain stored in our evidence vault," said Reardon.

"Oh, excuse me, I should have known," said Dunstan. "My thoughts are somewhat muddled."

"Back to your wife's drives in the country. Let's go over it again. Where might she have gone?" asked Maddingley.

"I have no idea. What about those areas I mentioned earlier? Have you gotten any leads from them?"

"No, nothing so far—no signs of her or the VW. We've been in contact with law enforcement in Lawrence County and talked to her cousins, but nothing's turned up. Were there any other places she was drawn to besides the ones you've already told us about?"

"I can't think of any."

"That's all we have today," said Maddingley. "Again, thanks for coming in and remember, contact us immediately if you hear from your wife or recall anything further, even if it seems unimportant."

Dunstan rose from his chair and stepped towards the door.

"Oh, one more thing," said Reardon. "Does your wife have a tattoo?"

"A tattoo? Certainly not! Why do you ask?"

"Lots of people have tattoos now and it's a standard question when we ask about physical descriptions of people."

"Thanks, that'll be all," said Maddingley.

Dunstan excused himself and left the room.

"Shouldn't we have gone ahead and arrested him?"

"Peggy, you know as well as I that we don't have a body and so far there's no clear motive—other than boorish behavior and a broken vase. Who knows? She might even still be alive."

"I don't think so. I can feel it in my gut. Something has happened to the real Belinda Dunstan and her husband is in it up to his eyeballs!" exclaimed Reardon.

"One thing seems certain, that woman in the video wasn't Dunstan's wife. I'm going to keep rechecking that new national tattoo database for behind the ear tattoos that begin with 'Ki.' It gets updated almost daily."

21

EDGAR DROVE INTO Whitby and stopped at a convenience store. *A few gallons for the truck and two six-packs and a sandwich for the belly,* he thought with a smile. *I'll bet those dumbasses in the hole would like some of this. Maybe I'll toss down a couple of beers in a few days, then again maybe I won't, 'cause there won't be none left.* He paid for his purchase and smiled as the teenage clerk leaned forward to pull a bag from under the counter, the top of her breasts briefly exposed. *Hey! I'll take a couple of those too!*

Oh, yeah, one more thing, almost forgot. He drove across town to a feed store. "Hey, Sammy, I need a couple of bags of that lime."

"You sure use a lot, does your garden need that much?"

"Well, it's useful for other things, but lately there's been a lot of dead skunks and sometimes a deer or hog gets hit on the road close to my fence. Lime helps keep down the flies and speeds up the rottin' but don't do nuthin for the odor. Kills a few buzzards who try to eat the carcasses but who cares? I don't like 'em hanging 'round."

"Well, they do help clean things up."

"Maybe so, but remember a few years ago when old

Pappy Helms dropped dead gettin' outta his truck. He was gonna put out hay for his cows. The old bastard lived alone so folks didn't miss him for a couple of weeks. The cows ate the hay out the back of the truck and the buzzards scattered him all over the place. That old pickup smelled so bad nobody even wanted to junk it for parts. They just left it out in that field. It's still rusting out there right now with briars and weeds growin' outta it!" *Yeah, gonna be two more dead skunks, but the buzzards won't get to 'em.*

As he drove by the cistern he honked a couple of times. *Hafta remind 'em who's boss 'round here.* The early evening air felt chilly when he got out of the truck. *How about a nice fire?* He dipped some kindling in kerosene and slipped the pieces under three logs over a small pit behind the trailer. He lit the kindling with his lighter and in moments it blazed. A quarter of an hour later the logs burned nicely. He plopped down in an old reclining lawn chair and popped open a beer.

God, a fresh opened beer and burning hickory, ain't nuthin much that smells better! He unwrapped and bit into the roast beef sandwich. The pungent taste of horseradish mustard filled his mouth. *We never got nuthin this good at Parchman Farm!*

"Dalton, we're going to seriously dehydrate pretty quickly. I lost a lot of fluid when I threw up. We need a hammer and chisel or a screwdriver."

"Sweetie, I just had a 'eureka moment'—my hiking boots! They've got a reinforcing shank in the sole. It's several inches long and high grade flexible steel. It'll make a great digging tool. If we can sharpen one end, it can be used like a chisel or gouge. I can use one of those bricks as a whetstone

145

and then as a hammer. But we need to be careful about breathing this lime dust. It's caustic and will damage our eyes and mucous membranes."

"Well, thanks for being concerned about my mucous membranes," she said with pointed sarcasm.

Dalton removed his jacket, shirt, and undershirt. He worked his fingers into a small hole in the undershirt and tore it in half. "There's no light so just go ahead and tie it over your whole face, eyes too. I'll do the same." It was almost chilly in the cistern. Dalton put his shirt and jacket back on and donned the half undershirt creating a crude facemask. It wasn't very effective, but it was better than nothing.

Removing the shank proved to be surprisingly difficult. He pulled off the considerably worn boots and examined their soles in the dark. They both seemed the same, but as he flexed them he could feel a split along the edge of the sole of the left one. "It's gonna take a while, but I think if we keep flexin' this boot, the sole will separate enough that I can pull out the shank. This steel's made to be flexible, so I don't think it'll break from metal fatigue."

Patiently he flexed the boot, bending it far more than his foot ever would in normal use. "Genn, try to rest while I do this."

"Okay but after a nap, I'll take over." She sat with her back against the chalk wall and prayed for deliverance from their predicament. *God, I beg you, please help us. If one of us has to die, let it be me. Keep Dalton safe.*

She thought of the little Methodist church she joined as a child and Mrs. Bonner, her Sunday school and fifth grade teacher who also lived next door. She often visited Mrs. Bonner and once confided that she hated her name and red hair because some of the children teased her, particularly Edgar who often shoved and sometimes even hit her when he thought no one was watching.

Mrs. Bonner hugged her and smiled. "Genevieve, you have a beautiful name. It comes from a young French woman who led a prayer vigil hoping to save Paris from Attila the Hun's army nearly sixteen hundred years ago. Her city was saved from destruction. Later she became Saint Genevieve, the patron saint of Paris. In French her name's pronounced 'ZAHN-vee-EHV.' Isn't that a *beautiful* story and name? Whenever someone teases you about your hair, just think of the first Queen Elizabeth, President Thomas Jefferson, and writer Tom Wolfe. Also Mary Magdalene from the Bible, for centuries artists have traditionally portrayed her with red hair. Always remind yourself how special it is to have something in common with such great people!"

Genn's lip no longer hurt and she drifted into sleep.

Dalton flexed the boot methodically at a measured pace. *One, two, three, bend.* His hands began cramping. *There has to be a better way.* He stood, held the boot's heel in both hands, and began pushing the toe against the wall. At intervals he stopped and felt the edge of the sole. The split seemed to be lengthening, but he wasn't sure. They had been expensive and were made to last. *How ironic, I bought these boots for their durability and now I'm trying to destroy one of them.*

A couple of hours had seemed to pass when Genn awoke. "Making progress?"

"Maybe, but it's a slow job."

"Give it to me, your turn to nap. Dang Dalton! The

smell down here is bad enough! When we get outta this mess, you're gettin' new boots."

"If that shank works I'm gonna have these old ones bronzed!"

Dalton sat down with his back against the wall, arms clutching his aching body. It was chilly in the cistern but sleep came quickly. He dreamed of being in his warm childhood bed and could hear his mother trying to wake him for breakfast.

"Dalton, Dalton," Genn said touching his shoulder, "I think the sole is starting to separate. See if you can pull it further apart."

Indeed the separation in the sole extended from near the heel to the toe. Inserting his fingers he could feel the shank. He gripped the sole and pulled with both hands. Gradually increasing the pressure, he felt the gap widening. Now he could flex the shank sideways to loosen the glue holding it in place. With surprising ease the shank slipped from side to side and with a gentle tug came free. The piece of steel was about three-quarters of an inch wide and maybe six inches long with slightly rounded ends. It wasn't very thick, about like the blade of a dinner knife.

"Here Genn," he offered it to her in his open hand. He reached for one of the broken bricks. "I'm gonna sharpen one end. See if you can sleep some more while I work on it."

Dalton pushed the shank across the surface of the brick producing a soft repetitive scraping sound. He remembered what his grandfather told him about sharpening chisels. *Hold the blade at about thirty degrees and push forward and back, over and over.*

Surprisingly soon a bevel began to develop on the end of

the shank. After twenty minutes he had a respectable edge. *Not bad, not bad, now we have a tool!*

He hated to wake Genn but felt they needed to get to work quickly. "Genn, let's get to work with this. Where's the best spot to start digging?"

She took the shank from him. "Hmm, it's fairly sharp, think it'll cut into the chalk?"

"Well, we have to try. I'm sure it will, but we'll probably have to sharpen it frequently since the chalk has a lot of silica in it and that'll dull the edge."

They ran their hands over the almost vertical face of the rough chalk. "I think there's a crack or joint running diagonally across here," he said. "Remember that chalk quarry outside Whitby we went down into that time? It had cracks like this. I think it would be easier to start the first holes along here."

She felt along the crack and chose a spot about knee high above the top of the pile of mostly desiccated and skeletonized bodies. "Start here Dalton," she said guiding his hand. "This seems to run upwards from left to right. Make the second hole on the right into the crack at that point. Then we'll continue on up diagonally."

"What's the best shape to make?"

"Like a stirrup on a saddle, rounded on top and flat on the bottom. Cut down from above and stop at the top of the bottom half of the crack. That way we can save a lot of cutting. That's what the ones at Acoma Pueblo looked like."

Dalton guided the shank with his left hand and applied force with his right. The sharp end dug into the soft chalk and he began removing about a sixteenth of an inch of material with each stroke. *Blisters—slow down and ease up or I'll get blisters. Wait a minute—I forgot to use that piece of brick as a hammer!*

Tapping filled the cistern and gradually the hole enlarged. "Genn put your foot here, is this deep enough?"

"I can get the tip of my shoe in but it's gotta be big enough for yours too. Make the hole more like a semi-circle on top so a shoe fits better." The old Fats Waller song, "Your Feet's Too Big," no longer seemed funny.

An hour or more passed. He stuck his left foot in the enlarged hole and it supported him when he pushed up with his full weight.

"Now dig here," said Genn guiding his hand to the spot.

"Okay, but first I need to sharpen this thing." He was surprised at how long the edge had lasted. After a couple of minutes the shank was ready to use again. Dalton settled into a steady rhythm chiseling out a new hole. Hours seemed to pass. There were now two holes—the highest about three feet above the top of the corpses.

Genn stepped up with her left foot and then raised her right into the second hole. "This just might work!"

"There's still a long way to go," said Dalton, "I'll start on the third hole. But we're gonna get too high to reach it from where we're standing."

Genn paused for a moment. "We're moving to our right as we go up. Reach back to the left and dig a handhold, it doesn't need to be as big or deep as the hole for our feet. That way we can hang on with our left hand while we dig to the right but we'll hafta stop using that brick. Take a break and I'll do the next hole."

Again Dalton restored the edge of the shank. He handed it back to her and sat with his back against the wall of the cistern. He adjusted the torn shirt covering his mouth and nose. Remembering one of Genn's relaxation techniques, he eased his body parts in sequence—first his toes, then feet, ankles, shins, knees, and up his body until he lay limp. Staring ahead he thought he discerned a faint dark shape— like a hooded, robed figure—against the opposite wall. As the minutes passed the figure seemed to raise its hand and make a slow sweeping gesture. On the floor a disarticulated foot seemed to move until it connected to an ankle. The ankle connected to a shin. Within moments the cistern came alive with writhing bones and body parts. One by one the skeletonized and partially-decomposed bodies rose from the floor. Their flesh and features began to return. They stood erect and faced Dalton. The eyes of the robed figure glowed and the word "behold" whispered in Dalton's mind.

"Uhhhhhhh," he moaned.

"What's wrong?" asked Genn from above.

"I'm okay, just an old dream returned for a moment."

"Another nightmare?"

"You could call it that."

22

DETECTIVE MADDINGLEY HAD developed a distinctive case of heartburn—too much coffee, three glazed donuts, and not enough sleep. A brief bathroom break and a couple of antacid tablets gave some relief.

Again he accessed the national tattoo data base. He had searched it at least once a day for the last week. So far his searches for behind the ear tattoos beginning with the letters "Ki" or something similar such as "Hi" or "Mi" had mostly yielded Hispanic gang members. The few females he found did not fit the physical description. They were either too short, too heavy, or a different race plus many were presently incarcerated.

With some frustration he used some of the same search terms and sorted the results by most recently listed.

"Peggy, look at this. Here's a woman in Walker County with a behind the ear tattoo—Kicky Harris—and she died a few days ago in a trailer fire."

"How did she get in the database?" asked Reardon.

"Arrest for possession of prescription opiates, happened a couple of months ago. Here, take a look."

Reardon sat down beside him and turned the screen

towards her. "With sunglasses and a scarf she could pass for Belinda Dunstan. In the video when she returns from the party, the light's too dim to see her very well. But Sunday afternoon when she drove away in that convertible the upper part of that tattoo's clearly visible."

"Also I looked at the profile mugshot side-by-side with the Facebook photo from the engagement party and the profile of the driver of Belinda's convertible. It's hard to tell, but it looks like the mugshot and the driver's image could match, especially the tattoo. I'd like another photo or two but at this point I'm thinking Kicky Harris could have been Belinda Dunstan's double," said Maddingley. "I'm gonna call the sheriff's office in Walker County and see if any female firefighters were on scene."

Moments later he hung up his phone. "Bingo! The sheriff's office over there says that a volunteer fireman named Mona Abbington worked the fire that killed our Kicky Harris!"

"Mona, tell us about what happened the night of that fatal trailer fire," said Maddingley.

"I got the call late, about midnight, and drove over quick as I could. Got there in maybe ten minutes."

"What did you see when you arrived?"

"The fire had pretty much choked itself off—burned up all the oxygen in the trailer. Still lotsa smoke though. Danny knocked open the door and while Jeff was getting ready to turn on the hose, we went in on respirators lookin' to see if anyone was in there. We could hardly see anything but we found her on a couch near the front door. We carried her out and started CPR, but I don't think she was still alive. Anyway the ambulance got there and took her to the hospital in Jasper. A doctor there pronounced her dead."

"What did you do after the ambulance left?"

"Danny and Jeff dragged that couch outside, it had been on fire. But it was probably more of a slow smoldering fire with lots of smoke and fumes. I went to tearing it apart and hosing it down to make sure it wouldn't start burnin' again."

"Did you see anything in or near that couch, anything out of the ordinary?"

"No, not really, just an ashtray and her drug stuff on the floor."

"Mona, are you sure there wasn't anything else?"

"Like what?"

"Jewelry perhaps, maybe a ring? We have reason to believe that a ring was taken from the scene of that fire and sold at a pawnshop in Birmingham. The owner described someone much like you. In fact he mentioned she was wearing a dark blue shirt with a firefighter's emblem, just like the one you're wearing today."

She paled and felt faint. *Oh crap!*

"What do you know about the ring in this photo?" asked Reardon. "Think carefully before you answer, it may be connected to a homicide."

Mona Abbington sighed deeply. "I was pulling that couch apart and there it was. I put it in my pocket, not thinking it was real. Later that evening I discovered it was. So the next day I took it to a pawnshop in Birmingham. Look officers, I'm sorry I took it but I'm a single mother and really needed that money."

"Do you know anything about Kicky Harris?" asked Maddingley.

"Just that she waited tables and lived in that beat up old trailer with her boyfriend. Also I heard she got in some trouble a few weeks ago—maybe drugs."

"Remember anything else about her?"

"Yeah, she had her name tattooed behind her left ear. She looked really bad when we pulled her outta that trailer but you could still see it."

"Peggy, the autopsy photos of Kicky Harris just came in. It's gonna take a while but I'm gonna do some more comparisons with that security video and the mugshots from the tattoo data base."

Maddingley pulled up a still shot of the convertible driver from the security video and compared it side-by-side with the mugshot profile and one of the autopsy photos of Kicky Harris. The similarity was striking. *I'm gonna overlay these the old fashioned way. I just don't trust facial recognition software.*

Maddingley printed scaled copies of the photos so that reference points such as the tips of noses and chins and the partially uncovered tattoo could be aligned. Using an X-ACTO knife he cut out profiles of the various images and overlaid them.

"Well whadda you know!"

"Whatcha got?" asked Reardon.

"That waitress was about twenty years younger than Belinda Dunstan but had about the same build. With sunglasses and a scarf I think she could pass for her. When she returns from the party, the light's too dim to see her very well. But Sunday afternoon when she drove away in that convertible part of that tattoo is clearly visible. But here's the clincher! Look at the cutouts of her profiles from the mugshot and the autopsy photos. They match the person in the security video. Then I overlaid these three matching profiles with the Facebook photo of the real Belinda Dunstan taken at the party. They don't match! Ergo … Kicky Harris was Belinda Dunstan's double!"

23

GRADUALLY OVER THE hours, the line of footholds extended further across the cistern wall. Her crude facemask slipped down. *I can see a faint light through that nail hole in the tin. It must be early morning.* "Wake up Dalton, your turn." She began coughing as she stepped down.

"How are your hands?"

"I wrapped a sock around the shank but there's a blister on the inside of my thumb where the edge of the shank rubs and one is forming in my palm. But I can deal with it. My left hand is okay."

"Get some sleep."

"Okay but first hold me, it's chilly down here." Dalton picked up his jacket and wrapped her torso. He sat with his back against the wall enfolding Genn in his arms until she fell asleep.

That's not much cover, but it's better than nothing.

Darkness engulfed Genn—a soft moist darkness almost like a silent nighttime fog. She felt the presence of someone near, comforting and familiar. "Genn, Genn," whispered a soft voice. She couldn't tell where the voice came from. Was it in her head or just feet away? There was no light or tunnel like she had read about in descriptions of near death experiences—just the soft voice—her mother's voice.

Mama, I'm scared. Then she knew her predicament to be like a cross-country race when she neared exhaustion and the end seemed so far away and the other runners steadily gaining ground. She had looked inside and felt it deep within—the will to go on. But doubt surrounded her now. The thought they may never escape and would spend eternity in this mass grave with those strangers, far from her family.

Stay calm. Stay in control. Don't panic! She knew she had to work methodically, plan ahead, and when the time came she would with all her strength do what was necessary to save them both.

Oh Mama, I miss you. There was no answer—only silent darkness.

The summer session at the University of Alabama began just days earlier. Students sauntered into a second floor classroom for the daily meeting of CE419, Rural Water Supply Engineering. It was eight o'clock. They chatted about the assignment due that morning and the impending weekend. A few minutes passed but Dr. Randolph did not appear.

Strange, thought Abigail Wallace sitting on the front row. *He's always a few minutes early.*

Some of the students began chatting while others worked on assignments for later classes. The clock reached fifteen minutes past the hour. "I'm going to check at the office," said Abigail.

"Mrs. Moore, has Dr. Randolph's class been cancelled? He hasn't shown up yet."

"He's not here? That's odd. I'll call his cell." After a few rings the call rolled to voice mail.

"I'll try his wife's department in Human Environmental Sciences."

Mrs. Moore's brow knitted as she talked with her counterpart across campus. "Now I'm getting concerned. She didn't show up for her eight o'clock either."

She entered her department head's office. "Neither Dr. Randolph nor his wife came in this morning and I can't reach them on their cell phones."

"That's alarming, Linda—not like either of them. They don't have a land line at home as I recall."

"No, they don't, but maybe a text can reach them, sometimes those will go through when coverage is bad." Again there was no response.

"Yesterday Dalton said they were going down to Hastings' Fish Camp in Tombigbee County for lunch since neither had classes after eleven."

"Linda, I'll call down there and see if they know anything."

He checked his contacts list and found the number. "May I speak to Lowrene Latham?"

"You've reached the one and only!"

"Sorry Lowrene, I didn't recognize your voice. This is Leo Shaffner in Tuscaloosa. We met last year when Dalton and Genn Randolph brought my wife and me down there."

"Oh yeah, you're Dalton's boss, the good-lookin' bald-headed guy. What's up?"

"Were they there yesterday?"

"Sure were … is sumthin wrong?"

"Neither showed up for their classes this morning and we can't contact them."

Lowrene gasped audibly. "Oh Lord! Could sumthin have happened to them?"

"I sure hope it hasn't. What should we do?"

Lowrene thought for a moment. "I'll call the sheriff here. Do you know any of their neighbors?"

"No, but I'll go over right now and see if they're home."

Shaffner drove to Dalton and Genn's neighborhood across the river. Their driveway was empty and no one answered the doorbell. He walked across the lawn to the houses on both sides, but no one was home. Back at the Randolph's he stood on his tip-toes and peered into one of the garage door windows and saw the top of Genn's Subaru. *Now I'm really worried.*

"Sheriff's Office."

"Lemme speak to Sheriff Mosby."

"One moment please."

"Mosby," he said with a slow drawl that stretched out the first syllable.

"Herb, this is Lowrene at the Fish Camp. I'm worried about Dalton and Genn Randolph. They came in for lunch yesterday and then said they were headin' home. Dalton's boss called and neither of them showed up at the University this mornin' and they aren't answering their phones."

"Hmmm, there haven't been any accidents since that time and as far as I've heard there've been no ambulance runs except one to the other end of the county that turned out to be a false alarm."

"Herb, I'm scared."

"Don't worry I'm sure they're okay. Tell you what; Lucius is on patrol not far from y'all. I'll have him retrace the route they probably took. Meanwhile I'll have one of the office staff call their relatives. Maybe they broke down and stayed with some of them."

"Let me call Hartwell. I'm one of the few people he's comfortable talkin' to. Even after five years he's still in deep mourning for Willie."

"Okay, but do it right away. I'll follow up in a little while."

"I can't believe they'd do sumthin like that and not let people know."

"We've gotta start somewhere Lowrene. We'll find 'em."

Dalton carefully ascended the wall. Seven steps had been carved into the chalk—the highest perhaps a little over ten feet above the floor. Adding his six-foot height he could almost reach the roof of the cistern near the edge of the entrance hole. He gripped the handhold to the left and started an eighth step. Progress was agonizingly slow and after about twenty minutes, his left hand was numb and the balls of his feet ached. Unconsciously he had been gripping the handhold too tightly. *Relax but don't let go.* He paused and waited for feeling to return.

"How's it going?" Genn's voice was faint and raspy.

"Slowly, but I'm making progress. Please try to rest some more. I'm okay."

He continued scooping out the hole. *It seems large enough.* He reached back to the left and started another handhold. It had to extend two or three inches into the wall and then down so his fingers could get a grip. The chalk seemed a little softer.

He slipped the shank into his pocket and gripping both handholds moved his feet. *My head's almost in the entrance hole!* The slender ray of sunlight projecting through the nail hole pointed almost straight down. *No need to check the cellphone. It's about noon Friday. We've missed our classes.*

In the distance he could hear the old pickup approaching. The brakes squeaked as it came to a stop. "Oh Dawt'un, Dawt'un, save me Dawt'un! I fell down a hole and I can't get out!"

"You sorry-ass son-of-a-bitch," mumbled Dalton.

"What was that?" moaned Genn as she sat up.

"Just a bad dream, please go back to sleep."

Deputy Lucius Jones left the Hastings' Fish Camp parking lot and turned left onto Alabama Highway 12. The roadway was elevated several feet. He drove slowly, scanning the pavement and roadsides. There were no skid marks and recent heavy rains had softened the shoulders and embankment. Any car leaving the pavement would leave deep muddy ruts. Nothing could be seen but a few wildflowers, grass, and scattered litter.

He drove by the cemetery, church, and old elementary school and turned left on Highway 95 towards Whitby. After passing through the line of hills that crossed the county, the countryside became open with pastures on either side of the road. However in many areas cedars growing along the fence lines obscured the view. But again nothing—no ruts, broken branches, or freshly scarred tree trunks.

In the distance to the northwest, he could see the limp red air sock at the Schroader Farm Airstrip. He drove past the entrance gate to Edgar Wellton's place. *Nothing here to see.*

Approaching Gum Pond Creek, he turned on his emergency lights and parked on the wide shoulder of the new bridge. Recent rains had swollen the normally shallow stream. This was a special place. He and Dalton spent many spring and summer days fishing and sometimes seining for crawfish and minnows. Once they abandoned their efforts after netting a small water moccasin. Both lay laughing on the creek bank holding their bellies as each joked about the other's reaction to the poisonous reptile.

But reality intruded upon his recollections. Peering over the guardrail at the rapidly flowing muddy water, he shuddered to think they might have driven into it. *Dear Lord, don't let them be down there!* He carefully examined the bridge approaches—no skid marks or rutted tire tracks. *That's a relief!*

He continued past the old Gum Pond Elementary School where he and Dalton spent many a boring day when they would rather have been hunting, fishing, or gadding about the countryside. Briefly reminiscing, he recalled that his biggest problem at that school was the windows—big windows with great views of the open pasture and woods where he wanted to be instead of memorizing the names of Alabama's sixty-seven counties and their county seats. He never could remember which two counties had two county seats each. Crossing Chulahomma Creek he entered the outskirts of Whitby and drove past the courthouse guarded by a marble Confederate soldier standing ever vigilant, looking north, his face obscured by a century and a half of mildew and lichens. He continued to the Tuscaloosa County line. Nothing seemed out of the ordinary. *Where can they be?*

"Three-twenty-one."

"Go ahead Lucius."

"I've checked all along the route they might have taken back as far as the county line and can't see any sign of that missing couple or their truck."

"Boss said to come in."

"On the way."

24

A PICKUP TURNED slowly into southbound traffic on Metropolitan Parkway in the Adair Park Neighborhood of Atlanta. Half a block behind, a fast moving MARTA bus approached. The bus driver yawned, shook his head, and blinked his eyes. *These days are gettin' too long and that pickup's movin' too slow,* he thought overtaking it.

Suddenly a kid on a bicycle sped from a side street half-hidden by overgrown bushes and into the path of the pickup. "Shit," hissed the driver of the pickup as he swerved sharply to his left. He missed the kid but was broadsided by the bus and pushed nearly half a block. The bicyclist fell but jumped to his feet, picked up the bike and fled with two pursuers close behind.

The impact threw the pickup driver violently to one side, his collar bone breaking as the shoulder harness locked and restrained him. Because of the angle of the collision the air bag did not deploy. He immediately lost consciousness. The passenger side door flung open and Tillman Coffee, aka "Hot," ran away limping and turned down a side street. He stopped at a small neighborhood park to catch his breath. In the distance he heard the wail of emergency vehicles. He calmly began walking toward his own neighborhood about ten blocks away.

—m—

"Gabe, didja hear about that MARTA bus hittin' a pickup last night?"

"Naw, I went to bed early and missed the local news. What about it?" he asked yawning.

"A dead guy was found in the truck, but the accident didn't kill him."

"Yeah, tell me more."

"The emergency folks found him in a body bag covered with plywood scraps in the back." Hilbertson took another sip of coffee. "He was killed execution style, shot in the back of the head/neck area with a small weapon, maybe a twenty-two or twenty-five."

"Fascinating," deadpanned Garland arching his eyebrows.

"Enough with the Spock imitation," groaned Hilbertson. "We got a preliminary ID from a mugshot—Erasmus Rogan, street name 'Flick.' He was a mid-level drug distributor just like our missing 'Six-Bits' Bateman. He was one of those rumored to be skimming too much. Forensics is going over the truck right now."

"Let's go take a look."

"Bobby, what can you tell us so far?" asked Hilbertson.

"Not much really. The guy didn't have a cell phone, jewelry, etc. He didn't bleed, the bullet didn't exit and someone put a bandage over the entry wound—must've been a small caliber. The body bag he was found in is standard issue for most agencies, mortuaries, etc. They're not very expensive and can be bought off the Internet. It has a manufacturer's tag and lot number, but I doubt that will tell us much. It could have been taken from almost any hospital or emergency service outfit."

"Anything interesting in the truck?"

"In the back some scrap plywood and a few clumps of pine straw covered the bag, but pine trees are everywhere around here."

"Any idea where they were headed?"

"Southbound on Metropolitan but coulda been headed anywhere—maybe somewhere less crowded where a body could be dumped. It'd be hard to discretely dispose of a body in Metro Atlanta, just too many people. There's a couple of old state highway maps in the glove compartment—Georgia and Alabama. But both are unmarked. My guess, and this is pure speculation, is that they were headed for Alabama. Somewhere like the Talladega National Forest or some remote rural area. We did find some dried mud on the underside of the truck."

"Interesting."

"I can't recall seeing anything like it. Soil samples go to a special consultant. He's retired from the Natural Resources Conservation Service, that's the old Soil Conservation Service. They have an office in almost every county seat."

"I'd like some quick answers to keep the ball rolling," said Garland.

"You know how it is with the 'Chain of Custody' for evidence, however, this is a large sample. We can give you part of it and the rest we'll formally submit with all the paperwork to Dr. Vincent for his 'official' exam and report. He'd probably be amenable to some preliminary comments—'off-the-record' of course. I'll text his contact info in a few minutes."

"First let's go talk to the driver at Grady Memorial. Then we can see 'Dr. Dirt.'"

Grady Memorial Hospital's large complex sat in downtown Atlanta near Interstates 75 and 85 and primarily served Medicaid and indigent patients. Detective Garland knocked gently on the door of a room on the seventeenth floor. As they entered an elderly woman rose.

"He's not supposed to have any visitors," she said softly as they displayed their badges.

"Sorry ma'am, this is Detective Hilbertson and I'm Detective Garland with the Atlanta Police. We need to ask a few questions. What is your relationship to Mr. Monro?"

"I'm his grandmother, Vileetta Monro. But like I said, he's not allowed visitors!"

"Sorry, but this is part of a police investigation. His physician said we could have a few minutes."

"Mr. Monro, we're investigating your accident. Tell us what happened," said Hilbertson.

Ulysses Monro lay in a hospital bed, his neck and shoulders encased by a formidable looking brace—his eyes badly bruised. "I was taking some plywood to my Grandma's house to fix her garage. I don't know what happened or how I got here," he said barely above a whisper.

"A witness said you swerved to miss a child on a bicycle and got rammed by a MARTA bus."

"I did? Is the kid okay?"

"Apparently you didn't hit him, but he left in a hurry since he was being chased. Who was with you in the truck?"

"Nobody, I was alone."

"Nobody? A witness saw someone jump out and run away."

"As far as I can remember, I was alone."

"No, Mr. Monro, you were not alone," said Garland. "There were three people in your truck."

"Whadda you mean?"

"The dead guy in the back—the one in the body bag."

"All I had in the back was plywood!"

"Oh Lord!" cried his grandmother. "You're tryin' to accuse him of murder. My Ulysses was on his way to my house to repair my garage! He would never be involved in anything like that, why he even sings in our church choir!"

"Mrs. Monro, please let your grandson answer our questions."

"I'm sorry detectives. I don't know anything about a body."

"Is that a fact? Well, you aren't under arrest, but there'll be a guard outside."

"We'll be back, Mr. Monro," said Hilbertson as they left.

"Good morning Dr. Vincent, thanks for seeing us on such short notice. I'm Gabe Garland and this is my partner Kenny Hilbertson."

"Gentlemen, how can I help you?"

"This dirt came from the underside of a pickup that's involved in an investigation. Can you tell us anything about it?" asked Garland.

"Perhaps," he said. "Can I open this and remove some?"

"Of course," answered Hilbertson. "The remainder of

the sample with a formal chain of custody will follow for your detailed examination and report. We need some 'off-the-record' comments to keep things going."

Vincent removed a fragment, rolled it between his fingers, smelled it, and examined it with a small pocket magnifying glass.

"This didn't come from around here."

"Why is that sir?" asked Garland.

"I haven't seen soil like this since I did field work forty years ago out of Auburn University over in Alabama. This is an 'udert,' a type of vertisol soil."

"Sorry, Professor, we're cops not soil scientists. Say that in plain English."

"Look closely, see these little white specks? Those are chalk fragments. This soil developed on an outcropping of chalk, a type of very soft limestone. It shrinks when dry and swells when wet. In summer it cracks wide open and in winter turns to sticky mud. It's a rather rare soil type, only found a few places in the world. I'd say this came from Alabama or perhaps even east Mississippi."

"Can you be more precise?" asked Hilbertson.

"Sure, probably west central Alabama, maybe Sumter, Marengo, or Tombigbee Counties, maybe even Noxubee County, Mississippi—just across the state line. That area is part of the Black Belt Prairie. When we did field work over there in wet weather, our vehicles and the bottoms of our boots would be caked with this stuff. The locals call it 'gumbo mud.'"

25

"DR. DUNSTAN, BEFORE beginning this interview Detective Maddingley will read a statement."

"Have you found my wife, is she alive?"

"You have the right to remain silent. Anything you say can and will be used against you in a court of law. You have the right to an attorney. If you cannot afford an attorney, one will be provided for you. If you understand, please review this acknowledgment form and sign it at the bottom."

"What ... what is this? Are you arresting me?"

"Dr. Dunstan, before we go any further with this interview you must clearly understand the statement I just read and sign the acknowledgment. Must I read it again?"

"I don't understand, what's happening?"

"Dr. Dunstan before we ask any questions, you must clearly understand that you are a suspect in the disappearance and possible murder of your wife, Belinda Dunstan. This interview is being recorded and anything you say, any questions you answer can and will be used against you in court. You have the right to have an attorney present. If you can't afford an attorney, one will be provided. Do you understand?"

"I understand that part, what I don't understand is what's happening."

"I repeat! You are a suspect in the disappearance and possible murder of your wife. You have the right to have an attorney present before you make any further statements or answer any of our questions."

"I'm not signing anything and I want to call my attorney."

"Okay, this interview is terminated. We'll leave the room while you contact him."

Reardon and Maddingley closed the door behind them. "Let's get a cup of coffee."

"I almost busted out laughing when you said, 'If you can't afford an attorney,'" said Reardon as they headed towards the break room.

"Think it's a good idea to read him his rights before an arrest?"

"I don't know who his lawyer is, but I'm sure he's a slick one, probably a golfing buddy. We need to be super careful with procedure. If it goes to court this might be the 'trial of the century' around here."

"Hartwell, this is Lowrene at the Fish Camp."

"Hey Lowrene, how's business?"

"Have you heard from Genn or Dalton recently?"

"Yeah, yesterday mornin', Genn invited me to meet them for lunch but I had to meet the vet to have my cows checked out. Why, what's going on?"

"Genn and Dalton had lunch here yesterday, but looks like they didn't get back to Tuscaloosa."

"What? Are you sure?"

"Dalton's boss called me and neither of them showed up for their eight o'clock classes this mornin'."

"What coulda happened?"

"I don't have any idea. Lucius came by a minute ago and is searching the way back right now."

"That concerns me."

"I'm sure Mosby will call you in just a little while. I wanted to let you know in advance."

"Thanks Lowrene, I'm gonna start lookin' too. Mosby has my cell number. Call me if you hear anything."

Oh no! What's my girl gotten into? Where do I start looking? If they were going straight back to Tuscaloosa, they'd have taken Highway 12 to Coleman's Corner and turned north on 95.

Hartwell Hastings turned his truck around and drove to the pasture's entrance. He locked the gate behind him and drove towards the river. At Coleman's Corner he looked carefully for signs of the white Tahoe and continued on past the Methodist Church. *Oh Willie, honey, where could they be? Think, Hartwell, think.*

A few miles before the river, he passed a slow moving sheriff's patrol car. *That must be Lucius. Hope his eyes are better than mine.*

He drove up to the Fish Camp and Lowrene waved from the porch. She ran out to his truck. "Lucius just left, said he's gonna check as far as the county line along 95 and that they'd notified the Tuscaloosa County Sheriff's Office."

"Thanks Lowrene, I'm gonna follow Lucius and start calling some relatives. Call me if you hear anything!"

Hartwell Hastings lived alone in the rambling 1902 farmhouse built by his grandfather. For years it was filled with laughter and constant activity. But his daughters moved away over a decade earlier and Willie died from a lingering bout with cancer. He still kept a herd of cattle, but leased the catfish ponds to a nearby Mennonite family. Now he spent most days alone.

"Lillian, did you hear from your sister yesterday or today?"

"No Pop, what's wrong?"

"She and Dalton are missing. They didn't show up at the University this mornin'."

"She called last week, but I haven't heard from her since. Do you think something bad's happened?"

"Lil, I just don't know. Where are you now?"

"Actually we're at Gulf Shores. Jake and I came over for a three-day weekend."

"I'm driving up 95 towards Tuscaloosa right now. Do you have numbers for any of Genn and Dalton's friends?"

"Not any of the ones in Tuscaloosa, but I have a call list for kids we went to high school with who are still around. I can start calling them right now."

"Good, good, you do that and I'll call some of the family here. Let's ask everybody we call to contact others. Maybe they dropped in on someone or had car trouble or became ill."

"Oh Pop. I'm so worried."

"I am too, but right now we need to get as many people lookin' as we can."

"I love you Pop."

"I love you too."

Hartwell drove slowly, carefully scanning the sides of the road. *Damn it! I wish I had gotten new glasses!* Cars sped around him and several even honked in frustration in no passing zones.

"Hartwell, this is Jimmie. Lillian just called. What's this about Genn and Dalton being missing?"

"Yeah, they ate lunch at the Fish Camp yesterday but didn't show up for work this mornin'. I'm headed north on 95 checking out the roadsides. Lucius is somewhere up ahead."

"I'm on the way to the airstrip. Tony and I are gonna search by air. Have any idea where they were headed?"

"Lowrene said they left at about half past two yesterday headed back to Tuscaloosa—looks like they never made it."

"Tony thought we should start at the Fish Camp and look carefully in the tree line along the road. Then come back and work south on 95 and east on 12. What are they driving?"

"Their white Tahoe, I don't know the tag number but since they live in Tuscaloosa, it'll start with sixty-three. They have a green UA faculty parking tag but it may not be hanging from the mirror since they're away from campus."

"I'll be riding shotgun with Tony. Billie's gonna take her Ag Cat and fly a spiral search pattern starting over the Fish Camp. She can get a lot lower than we can. There'll be about nine more hours of daylight and we can cover a lot of ground."

"Jimmie, y'all be careful. Watch out for those new concrete power poles along 95, they're pretty high."

"Will do Hartwell. We've got a good chance of finding 'em if they're still in the county.

Hartwell Hastings approached the Tuscaloosa County line. *Did they get this far?*

Jimmie and Tony, the Schroader twins, and their older sister, Billie, operated a large farm and ranch northwest of Coleman's Corner. All three learned to fly as teenagers and had inherited their father's two planes—a Cessna 172 and a Grumman Super Ag Cat crop duster. Billie loved flying the agile Ag Cat and operated her own spraying service. She also picked up a few dollars scattering the cremated remains of people and occasionally their pets over the countryside. Her old boyfriend, Sherwyn, often teased her and referred to her business as "Billie's Aerial Burials."

At the Schroader Farm Airstrip Tony taxied the little Cessna onto the grass runway. He opened the throttle and they leapt ahead. The runway sloped downhill and there was a moderate headwind. Indeed, the rows of corn flashed by in a blur of green.

"What about the cows?" yelled Tony.

"I checked the fences yesterday. We don't need a fifteen-hundred-pound Black Angus for a hood ornament!"

Back at the airstrip Billie taxied her Super Ag Cat out of the hanger that had once been their grandfather's barn. With an empty hopper the plane was almost half its maximum takeoff weight. The six-hundred-horsepower radial engine roared as the little biplane shot like a yellow rocket into the morning sky. *Hang on guys, we're comin'!*

"Hartwell, this is Mosby. Have you heard from Lowrene?"

"Yeah, she called. I'm trailing behind Lucius. Billie Schroader and the twins are starting an aerial search."

"They're always so good about these sorts of things, just like their father."

"Jimmie and Tony are checking along the roads and Billie's gonna fly a search pattern spiraling out from the Fish Camp. Be honest with me Herb, what do you think happened?"

"I'd just be guessin' if I tried to answer that. Let's don't speculate. I know it's hard but let's search. Who knows? They may turn up five minutes from now."

"As long as they're alive, that's all I'm praying for."

The flight from the airstrip to the Fish Camp took only minutes. Billie banked steeply as Lowrene waved from the parking lot below. *Lord that gal can fly that little plane!*

Julie, a young waitress, came outside. "What's she doing Miss Lowrene?"

"She's cuttin' didos, honey!"

"Cuttin' didos, what's that?"

"Just an old expression. Ask your mama, she knows. Your generation spends too much time watching television and playing with iPhones."

Billie's path carried her over the Tombigbee River and she turned back and circled the restaurant and the cotton and soybean fields. *Nuthin unusual, just a few deer and a lotta crows.* Beyond the field lay Hastings Swamp, Billie watched her altitude carefully. Some of the ancient cypress trees stood over a hundred feet high. *Lotsa beaver lodges, a fast-flying pair of wood ducks, and that big old gator that helps keep down the wild hog population.*

North along Highway 95, Hartwell Hastings turned right unto a logging road littered with beer cans, household trash, and an old mattress. He got out and examined the rutted surface. *Nothing's been here since the rain last week.*

177

Further up the highway he came to another logging road, this one covered with a low growth of undisturbed pine seedlings and immature goldenrod.

Overhead Tony and Jim remained at about five hundred feet. They scanned the roadside fields and scattered patches of forest on the east side of the highway, but nothing out of place could be seen. Dozens of scrap vehicles and countless pieces of unrecognizable junk surrounded one house— *nothing drivable down there*. They reached Tuscaloosa County, turned around, and began a sweep down the west side of Highway 95. They passed over houses and mobile homes and saw countless vehicles but nothing that matched the Tahoe.

26

"GARLAND."

"Detective Garland, this is Sheriff Herbert Mosby in Tombigbee County, Alabama, returning your call."

"Thanks for calling me back Sheriff. We have a mystery over here in Atlanta that may be connected to your area."

"Tell me more."

"Yesterday a MARTA bus hit a pickup in south Atlanta. The investigating officers found a corpse in a body bag in the back. When our forensics people examined the truck they found soil on the underside that apparently came from the Black Belt. Our soil expert referred to it as 'gumbo mud.'"

"That's one thing we have in abundance. What about the corpse?"

"Young black guy named Erasmus Rogan—drug distributor with a long record. Someone shot him in the back of the head—small caliber, no exit wound. The entry wound was bandaged to prevent bleeding. There's another guy named Bateman who's missing. Both were in the same organization and reputed to be skimming. There's a possibility the driver and a passenger who ran away were gonna dump the body over there. Have y'all found any unidentified corpses?"

"No, but this would be the perfect place to dispose of unwanted bodies. We've got over a thousand square miles and only a few more than ten thousand people, nearly half are here in Whitby, the county seat. We haven't found any unidentified bodies in a long time. But we're lookin' for two people who went missing locally a few days ago. Also a high-profile woman from the Birmingham suburbs has been missing for over a month and there are suspicions of foul play. It's unusual for this area to have that many missing."

"If someone wanted to conceal a body over there, where do you think they might do it?"

"That's a good question—could be lotsa places—in the river, in the swamps, in old dug wells in the north part of the county, in a quarry or cistern in the prairie where it's shallow to chalk. For that matter they could simply dig a hole in the ground. But bodies have a way of reappearing. They might surface in the river or swamps. Someone might notice a freshly dug and refilled hole. I guess their biggest problem would be gettin' access to some land here unless there was a local collaborator. Almost all our property is fenced, gated, and locked since believe it or not; we have cattle rustlers and horse thieves that come through plus hunters who trespass."

"Sounds like searching over there would be quite a task."

"Actually we have a massive search underway at the moment. We've got a couple of local aircraft plus air units from Tuscaloosa and the Civil Air Patrol up, and dozens of people searching along the roads. Lotsa property owners are lookin' into every corner of their places. The missing are

University of Alabama professors and both have extended family down here. Even some of their students came down from campus and are out there right now. If they're here we're gonna find them."

"So far I've checked with law enforcement in several counties and even over into Mississippi. Not much is going on 'cept in your area. When the condition of the truck driver over here improves we'll be leaning on him pretty hard."

"Send us some photos and other information about that missing guy and we'll alert the searchers."

"Will do, good luck and hopefully we can get to the bottom of these cases soon."

"Lucius?"

"Go ahead Sheriff."

"Where are you?"

"Headed south on County 47, south of State 12."

"Meet me at Coleman's Corner A-S-A-P!"

"On the way."

Deputy Lucius Jones flipped on his light bar, turned around and headed back towards Alabama Highway 12. Suddenly a red and white MINI Cooper convertible flashed by in the opposite direction. Abigail Wallace and her roommate Cynthia Crosswhite had joined the search.

"I have no idea where we are," said Cynthia. "There's just no coverage out here and GPS looks wonky."

"That deputy knows sumthin! Watch this," exclaimed Abigail as she jerked the steering wheel left and pulled the handbrake. With tires screeching and Cynthia screaming, the MINI skidded sharply left as if it would leave the road but the rear end swung around neatly to the opposite direction in the other lane. Abigail accelerated hard and sped after the deputy at nearly a hundred miles per hour.

Cynthia gripped the seat and armrest so hard her hands turned white. "What did you just do?" she asked her eyes wide with fear.

"Bootleg turn, Daddy taught me ... said I needed to know how to get away quick if I was being followed or chased."

The MINI quickly overtook the patrol car and took a position less than a car length from its bumper. Lucius glanced in his rear view mirror. "What the hell?" He began to slow and turned into a parking lot at a country church.

Abigail skidded to a stop beside the patrol car door.

"Whadda you think you're doin'?" growled Lucius.

"Lookin' for the Randolphs."

"Driving like that's dangerous and you're interfering with police business!"

"We're just trying to help."

"Go to the courthouse back in Whitby, the searchers are coordinated outta there. Now stop following me and slow down or I'll arrest you for reckless driving!"

"I'm sorry," said Abigail sniffling in her little girl voice. Lucius sped away toward his meeting with the sheriff.

"Let's go to Whitby!" Abigail yelled as the MINI slung rooster tails of gravel and grit across the church parking lot and slid sideways onto the road. As she accelerated the tires spun on the asphalt and left a trail of blue smoke.

Cynthia sat pale with terror, her teeth tightly clenched. "Abby, I'm NEVER gettin' in a car with you again unless I bring an extra pair of pants. Now slow down! This road is dangerous!"

———⟋⟋⟋—

"Sherwyn?"

"This is he."

"Herb Mosby in Whitby."

"How's the search going?"

"Nothing so far but I just talked to a cop in Atlanta. They're missing a drug dealer over there and just found the body of another in a truck that had some of our gumbo stuck to its underside. He thinks someone might be disposing of bodies over here. We got to discussing it and the thought came to mind that if that's going on they would hafta have a local connection. Also it wouldn't be easy if you wanted the bodies to stay hidden without a trace."

"Think Genn and Dalton somehow got tangled up in it?"

"Could have. You know there's also the high-profile case of that missing Vestavia Hills woman. Seems to me they'd need an already existin' place that doesn't show any signs of disturbance—maybe an abandoned quarry or well, even an old cistern dug in the chalk."

"There're a number of old cisterns in the chalk areas. My uncle Llewellyn had one on his place. There was an old house out there that fell in many years ago. The cistern was right next to it, the entrance hole was, oh, maybe eighteen inches across. But down below it opened up really big, had a dome shape like a beehive. He hired a couple of foolhardy guys to go down in it. There was no water but they found a corroded Winchester Model 73 rifle."

"Yeah, I remember now. He hung it over his fireplace. Said it was probably a murder weapon since back then those things were very expensive and if it'd been accidentally dropped the owner woulda retrieved it. Is there any way to locate where those cisterns might be?"

"Actually I have some maps that show where most of the old houses out on the prairie used to be. I put it together for those engineers who were lookin' for that transcontinental pipeline route a few years back. Those people prefer to avoid historic sites so they don't hafta pay to have them excavated by archaeologists."

"Do you know which ones had cisterns?"

"No, but I could make a pretty good guess since most of those places were small farms or sharecroppers' shacks. They couldn't have afforded to have a cistern dug and likely would have used barrels to collect rainwater from their roofs."

"When can you have that?"

"Let's see it's about four o'clock. I'll work all night if I have to. So let's say late tonight or early in the morning. As soon as I have something, I'll drive it down to your office."

"Great! I'll let Billie Schroader know and have her on standby to fly over those places and see if there's been any activity. We'll check them out on the ground as quickly as we can."

"I can tell you right now where there's probably one— Edgar Wellton's place on 95. There's where Dalton thought he saw a body in the distance!" said Sherwyn.

27

IDIOT! IDIOT! IDIOT! How could I have been so stupid? Why couldn't I just leave things alone? Genn must really hate me. By God, she has reason to. Her life's at risk. My fault, my fault. Why didn't I listen? Self-loathing and recrimination gnawed at Dalton, his mind endlessly repeating the same thoughts. *We're gonna die. No one will ever know what happened to us. Stop it Dalton, keep going! You got her into this, now you gotta get her out!*

He continued scraping into the wall—fingers numb and legs threatening to cramp. Hours passed, but he had another step and handhold. *Gotta rest and check on Genn—dear sweet Genn. Are these our last days?* He backed down off the side of the cistern. Dust motes like tiny fireflies danced in the single ray of sunlight that slanted downward and faintly illuminated the upper part of the cistern. However, the shadows below loomed sinister.

The lime-covered corpses seemed to laugh. *They're mocking me for being such an arrogant fool. They had no choice but I did and I made the wrong one—stupid, stupid, stupid! We can't die like this but it looks like we will unless we can get out this way. Oh Genn, how can you ever forgive me? Hafta keep digging and scratching at this chalk!*

Genn stirred, "What time do you think it is?"

"I'm just guessin' but from the angle of the sun probably late afternoon, maybe sumthin like five—got an appointment?"

"Yep, with a gallon of water, a sack of Krystal cheeseburgers, and a long soak in a tub of hot water with a lotta Epsom salts."

"Sounds good—make that a tub for two. How do you feel?"

"Stiff and sore, but I'm ready to get back to work. When do you think Edgar will be back?"

"No way to tell, but since it's Friday, let's hope he's off somewhere drinking his paycheck."

Genn rose and stepped to the pile of corpses. *Wonder if the woman in the cocktail dress has a watch. Gross! I've almost gotten used to the smell, but at least her eyes are closed.* Genn brushed the lime away but Belinda Dunstan's wrists were bare. *I can't believe I'm reduced to scavenging from a dead person!*

"Let's get outta here and quick." She shuddered and slid the cellphone and shank into her pockets to climb. "Two more footholds and I think I can reach the top. Lemme check for cell coverage first."

"Any bars yet?" Dalton asked from below.

"One bar keeps blinking on and off. I need to get further up, but I did get the time, it's four thirty." Distressingly the sides of the entrance hole were beginning to taper inwards over Genn's head. "If I can get a little higher, maybe we can call, but the battery has gotta be close to dying."

A distant faint droning suddenly turned into a roar. *I*

know that sound, it's Billie Schroader's hot-rod crop duster. Maybe she's searching for us! "Dalton do you hear that?"

"I bet they're lookin' for us! That has to be Billie's plane. But there's no way she can tell we're down here. She might see that piece of tin roof but not the hole we're in. We've gotta keep digging!"

Genn furiously attacked an ancient pick mark. *We're gonna make it!*

Dalton slowly slid down against the wall, careful not to stir up the ubiquitous lime dust. His lips and tongue were swollen and his thirst ravenous. He could see Genn's silhouette above as she clung like a fly on the wall. *Oh God, how I love her. Please help us get out of this mess. Dear Lord—I beg You! Spare Genn. Forgive me for being so arrogant.*

His throat was raspy but his breathing became regular and he drifted into the semi-consciousness that lay between sleep and reality. Images filled his mind. He fell—fell from the top of the cistern. But felt nothing when he landed next to Genn's body—still, emaciated, and coated with lime dust. He lay beside her, dead too but aware of the others with them. He could hear them chanting in a whisper, "You did this, you did this."

Genn's body stirred beside him, she raised a shriveled arm and pointed—pointed at him. He couldn't breathe. He choked and coughed himself to consciousness.

"You okay down there?"

"Yeah, just this danged dust, I'm all right."

Genn returned to digging. *Don't panic, slow down. This is just like a distance race. Don't expend your energy too quickly. There's the finish line—just a few feet overhead!* She settled into a steady pace gouging out another foot and handhold. She thought of her mother and father and sister Lillian. Her mind drifted to her earliest memories—bright sunlight, light green grass and spring leaves, her sister laying on a blanket and her mother singing, the little Coleman's Corner Elementary School, her first grade teacher, and the first time she saw Dalton in the seventh grade.

But her thoughts darkened, Edgar lurked in the recesses of her mind, just as he often lurked behind the shrubs beside the front door of their school ready to lunge out and hit, shove, and taunt her. The worst of her childhood had returned—not as a nightmare but a real-life horror, a horror even worse than the pile of bodies. *We hafta get outta here and run as fast as we can!*

She fought panic and nausea, clinched her teeth, and kept digging. *Slow down Genn, slow down ....*

28

IT WAS LATE afternoon and Edgar approached the gate to his property. It had been a long workday and he looked forward to relaxing with a beer and sandwich. *What's this! Damn cops! Whadda they want?* Indeed two Sheriff's patrol cars sat beside his gate.

"Hello Sheriff, Deputy Lucius, what I can I do for y'all?"

"Routine visit," said Lucius, "we need to check out your place for your parole officer over in Meridian."

"Okay, come on in, but don't expect the trailer to be cleaned up for company," he said with a chuckle.

The patrol cars followed Edgar's truck through the gate.

In the distance they could hear the muffled rumble of an engine. "He's back," said Dalton, "get back against the far side in case he shoots down here or dumps another body!"

He pushed Genn against the wall and spread his arms protectively. "What are you doing?" she cried. "Just stay calm. He can't see us from up top if we stay back here!" She pushed him away from her. "Keep quiet and don't move."

As the vehicles got nearer they could hear tires crunching gravel. They didn't stop but headed on towards Edgar's trailer. "He's not alone, there're at least two other vehicles with him!" Dalton exclaimed.

The patrol cars and Edgar's old truck stopped at the dilapidated trailer. Edgar opened the door and the officers briefly looked around the filthy interior. One room served as kitchen and bedroom with a tiny bathroom to one side. All that could be seen were dirty clothes and fast food wrappers.

"There's no runnin' water?" asked Sheriff Mosby.

"That's right and there won't be as long as the county water system wants a five hundred dollar hookup fee to put a meter out there by the gate. Then I hafta pay for about half a mile of water line to get it here."

"How do you bathe and do laundry? What about flushin' the toilet?"

"There's a shower and laundry room at the garage where I work in Meridian. As for flushin' the toilet I fill the tank from that rain barrel outside. It collects runoff from the roof my uncle built over the trailer."

"Let's go outside and look around," said Deputy Lucius. The area surrounding the trailer was littered with abandoned farm equipment—old plows, a derelict Ford tractor, an ancient hay baler, and assorted unidentifiable junk.

"Looks like a tornado hit this place," said the Sheriff.

Edgar laughed out loud. "Well it did! About ten years ago one came through and wrecked an old barn, scattered tin and a lotta junk all over the place. My uncle was gettin' too old to clean it up. He salvaged some of it to build that shed over the trailer. I've done a little but I spend most of my time working in Meridian. Maybe one of these days after I'm off parole, I'll have enough money saved to buy a few head of cattle. Right now I lease the pasture rights on part of the place to the folks next door."

"Where was that old antebellum mansion that was out here?" asked the Sheriff.

"I really couldn't say. It burned down long before I was born and even before my uncle got the place. There's some old broken brick scattered here and there and some flowers that come up each spring but they're spread all 'round. I think my uncle and the banker that owned the place before him spread the ruins 'round to cover up some of the gumbo mud. Later my uncle dumped a lot of gravel out here to make the road passable in wet weather."

"Are there any old wells or cisterns out here?"

"You mean like a dug or bored well?"

"Yeah like that."

"Nobody would dig a well out here, hell; there ain't no groundwater in that chalk. There ain't no bored well neither, it'd hafta be a thousand feet deep to get below the chalk and into an aquifer. Or at least that's what my uncle told me."

"What about a cistern? Wouldn't the people who lived in that mansion have had one?" asked the Sheriff.

"Never heard of one out here, cattle and horses have been on this place forever. I'd bet if there had been one folks woulda covered it up or filled it in. An animal with a broke leg is worthless."

"We'll look around for a while before we go," said the Sheriff.

"Suit yourselves officers. In the meantime if you don't mind, I'm gonna have a couple of beers and a sandwich I picked up in Meridian. It's been a long day."

The Sheriff and Lucius walked around the area

surrounding the trailer. "Looks like there really was a tornado out here, I don't remember ever hearing about it."

"Well since it didn't get into town or hit any houses, people quickly forgot."

"Lucius, it's like lookin' for a needle in a haystack. The entrances to those old cisterns are only about a foot or two across and they may have trees or bushes growing over them. It'd be hard to spot a hole in the ground that small on a place this big."

"Hey Sheriff!" Edgar yelled from the trailer door, "Y'all ever find those two missin' people?"

"We're still lookin'. Have you seen or heard anything about 'em?"

"Naw, not at all, I remember them from high school. But don't recall ever seein' 'em since then. Hope y'all find 'em okay. Tell 'em I said hello if you do."

The patrol cars drove slowly towards the front gate, both officers carefully scanning the pasture on either side. They approached the ancient bodock tree with embedded barbed wire, the brush pile, and the piece of tin covering the cistern and its contents.

"That sounds like two vehicles, maybe cars, coming back by," said Dalton.

"Who do you think they could be?"

"Doesn't matter! Maybe they can hear us! HELP!" yelled Dalton. "HELP!"

"Somebody, help us!" shouted Genn. "We're down here!"

They yelled several more times but their throats were raspy and their voices weak. The sound of the cars faded.

Mosby stopped at the gate and radioed Lucius. "Drive on down to that little church just past the bridge, we need to talk."

The cars pulled into the parking lot of St. John's AME Church. "Whadda you think?"

"Sheriff, it's hard to say but I think Edgar's involved in sumthin. He wasn't mad or sulled up like usual. He seemed to be tryin' too hard to be nice."

"Agreed, but didja notice all those sheets of tin and other debris scattered all over the place? One piece of tin was even wrapped around the trunk of that big cedar just before that old bodock."

"I remember seeing that barn when I was in high school. It was huge and must've had hundreds of pieces of tin and now they're everywhere. It doesn't look like Edgar has tried to clean up that place one bit since he moved out here."

"If there's a cistern out here it's gonna be on the central part of the property since that's probably where the big house sat. But it's likely covered with that debris. As I recall, that house burned in the forties. The first aerial photos of the county were taken by the USDA in 1956, so trying to pinpoint it that way is out. It would take fifty to a hundred searchers a couple of days to cover that area and turn over every piece of tin and other junk."

"What about a cadaver dog like they use after disasters. They used them in Tuscaloosa after that big tornado a few years ago."

"That's a great idea but we'd need a warrant and I'm not sure we have probable cause yet. Dalton's the only one who thinks he saw a body out here and he's missing."

"Something is going on here—the body in that truck

in Atlanta with our mud on the undercarriage, Genn and Dalton missing plus the other Atlanta guy and that rich doctor's wife. Also remember Edgar pays his property tax with a big stack of small bills."

From above came the sound of Edgar's truck and then screeching brakes and squeaky door hinges. The piece of tin covering the hole slid aside and light glared into the cistern. "Having fun yet?"

They pushed themselves against the far wall of the cistern. "Edgar, please let us out," implored Genn.

"I don't think you killed any of these people," interjected Dalton. "Don't let us die down here and we'll do everything we can to help you in court. You're just an accessory at this point and if you tell everything you know there's a good chance you'll get a light sentence."

"You can forget that! There's no way I'm gonna go back to prison. And do you really think I would rat out my friends?"

"The authorities might get you into a witness protection program. The Feds'll probably be involved so you could start over in another state—maybe the West Coast or somewhere in the Rockies like Colorado or Idaho."

"Not a chance," laughed Edgar. "They wouldn't do sumthin like that for a guy like me. Besides my friends are all over the place. There ain't no place to hide."

"We've never done anything to you, don't make things worse," pleaded Genn.

"In the old days I coulda shot both y'all! Just why did y'all trespass out here."

"It's my fault," said Dalton. "A few weeks ago I took a

photo from the highway and when I looked at it later, I saw what I thought was a body laying out here on the ground. We drove by here again yesterday, and I thought you would be at work. Genn begged me not to do it, but I climbed over the gate anyway."

"Know what they say—'curiosity killed the cat!'"

"Please don't let us die down here."

"Sorry, but this conversation is over." Edgar slid the tin back over the hole. His truck started with a roar, but sat idling.

That asshole sheriff and his deputy are making me nervous. They're suspicious of sumthin. That Hastings bitch is right, I haven't killed anyone. Guess I'm an 'accessory after the fact.' Maybe being in a witness protection program wouldn't be so bad. I've always wanted to go out West. But the 'friends' are everywhere, they'd find me for sure and I don't wanna lose this land, it's all I got. Maybe I should keep 'em alive for a while so they'll be bargaining chips. But then again they have 'bout as much chance of findin' 'em as they do of findin' the Gondolier's Gold!

He reached behind the seat and found a plastic bag with a single bottle of water. He got out and approached the hole.

Hearing the truck door slam Dalton pushed Genn behind him and pressed her against the wall. Again the tin slid aside. "Heads up!" Edgar shouted as he slid the tin back over the hole.

Something heavy plopped atop the pile of corpses. "Don't tell me it's another body," moaned Genn.

Dalton carefully approached and felt around in the darkness. "It's a plastic bag, feels heavy like there's a bottle inside."

"Beer?"

"Beer doesn't come in plastic bottles." Dalton pulled out the bottle, but the light was too dim to see a label. The bottle was soft and had no internal pressure like a carbonated drink. "Sweetie, this must be water!"

"Don't drink it! Open it carefully and give it a sniff. Dab your finger in it and taste just a drop," said Genn.

"No smell. It's seems to be okay!"

"Oh, thank God, maybe he's having second thoughts."

"Or just toying with us, but whatever, let's get you rehydrated."

Genn took a tiny sip, just enough to wet her parched tongue and lips. "Here Dalton, your turn, take just a couple of sips."

It was the most exquisite tasting water he ever had in his mouth. "If we had thirty thousand more gallons we could swim out!"

"That's not funny. We have to ration this carefully. Let's finish this one and hope for another tomorrow. Remember just take little sips."

29

WITH LYNYRD SKYNYRD'S "Free Bird" filling her ears, Billie Schroader continued her spiral search pattern—a flight of wood storks scattering at the blare of her engine. She had been making a slow constant left turn for hours. Twice she returned to the airstrip to refuel. The landscape below glowed with a variety of lush greens and scattered outcrops of white chalk. The still catfish ponds and lakes mirrored the sky above and occasionally the sun reflected from the water's surface and glared directly into her cockpit. Sunglasses helped but still she winced at the brilliant flashes.

Whoa, watch it! She suddenly passed through a flock of vultures circling a writhing mass of their brethren on the ground.

Uh-oh, what are they onto? She pumped the fuel/air mixture control—a trick she learned from an old-time crop duster pilot who flew war surplus Stearmans. The engine backfired and the vultures scattered. She flew back over the spot.

The scavengers had rendered their meal unrecognizable. *I hafta put down.*

Billie carefully scanned the area. There were several

hundred acres of open pasture, traversed by a field road. *That's the Peterson Place. I should be able to land on that road.* She aligned the Ag Cat and landed about a hundred yards from the carcass.

Exiting the cockpit, she pulled a Glock from her shoulder holster and chambered a round. From the tree line came the sound of wild piglets. *Careful Billie, don't rush up on this too quickly, an old sow might come outta those woods hell-bent for yo ass!* She slowly approached the carcass while constantly scanning the area. The vultures and other scavengers had left little of the dead animal except bone and hide. The internal organs had been the first parts consumed.

Poor little calf, the coyotes must've taken you down. We've got to get better at taking out coyotes and wild pigs. Maybe trapping on a bigger scale would make a dent in 'em.

In the distance a horn sounded, a truck was headed across the pasture. "Hey Billie! What's going on?"

"Mr. Peterson, I'm searching for Dalton and Genn Randolph. They're missing. Buzzards were all over this calf and I couldn't tell what it was. I put down to check it out. Hope you don't mind."

"Not at all, I saw you circling a few minutes ago and got curious. You say Dalton and Genn are missing?"

"Yes sir, they came down to the Fish Camp yesterday for lunch and never showed up back in Tuscaloosa. We've got a search going. Word got out quickly and I'm sure a lotta folks are lookin' for 'em right now. My brothers are up running the roads and I'm spiraling out from the Fish Camp where they were last seen. Thank goodness this turned out to be a calf."

"There're just too many invasives—first fire ants now

coyotes and pigs. Those things just can't be killed fast enough."

"I don't know what we can do—maybe bigger catchment pens. I used to think aerial hunting would work, at least in the Black Belt where there's enough open land to be effective. But the sows just produce too many piglets. Anyway, I need to get back in the air. There's still several hours of daylight left."

"Well, get on back up there. In the meantime I'll get some help and we'll go over my place. There're some spots you probably can't see from the air. Be careful now."

Billie jogged back to her plane and quickly got airborne.

Her search now stretched several miles from the Fish Camp. She approached the river just above Lime Rock Landing. *What's that bluish-purple patch off the end of the boat ramp?* Billie turned back and flew as low as she dared, slowing to just above stall speed. *Watch out for those sycamores at the edge of the water.*

"Sheriff's Office."

"This is Billie Schroader. I'm over Lime Rock Landing and can see oil coming up … maybe forty to fifty feet off the end of the boat ramp. Water's too muddy or deep to see anything."

"Sheriff Mosby, Billie's calling from her plane, says she sees oil on the water off Lime Rock."

"Tell her we'll be there A-S-A-P!"

It took several dives in the fifteen-foot-deep water for three-hundred-pound "Shirtless Sam" Fischer to finally locate a D-ring on the rear bumper of a submerged vehicle and attach a towing hook. "Whew," he said almost breathless as he popped up and pulled off his face mask, "can't tell exactly what it is ... visibility's zero ... could be a heavy-duty SUV or truck."

Sam waded out and started the tow truck's winch. Hartwell Hastings stoically stood nearby with clenched teeth and tightly pursed lips. The winch whined and the tow truck lurched as the cable drew taut and slowly slid from the water. In minutes the muddy rear of a vehicle began to emerge.

"It's a Tahoe and the windows are down," shouted Sam as water gushed out. He squatted behind at the rear bumper and wiped away the mud with his hand. "Tag starts with sixty-three—Tuscaloosa County."

Hartwell Hastings took several steps forward. "That's Genn and Dalton's truck!"

"Wait a moment Mr. Hastings," said Deputy Jones. "Let me check it out." The deputy peered in the open windows of the partially filled SUV. "Nothing's visible so far Sheriff. Want me to open a door?"

"Go ahead."

The door opened easily and a wall of water poured out soaking the deputy's shoes and trouser legs. A couple of small fish flopped around on the boat ramp's concrete surface. "It's empty!"

"Oh thank God!" cried Hartwell Hastings as he sank to his knees. "They may still be alive!"

Mosby and his deputy stood staring at the SUV. "If Edgar's behind this, how could he have run that Tahoe off in the river here. He had to have help. It must be ten maybe twelve miles back to his place," said Lucius.

"Didja notice that bicycle leaning against the trailer? He coulda taken it with him. Almost nobody uses this landing anymore since the Corps of Engineers opened that new one with the recreation area north of Whitby. He coulda come over here at night and rolled the Tahoe in and just ridden that bike back. He coulda done it in an hour and a half or two hours. There ain't no steep hills between here and there—next to no traffic at night neither."

Two more footholds! She ached miserably. She gouged and scraped until her hands began to numb. "Watch out, I've gotta get down!" She fell the last few feet but he grabbed and caught her enough to slow her fall.

She gasped and trembled. "Gimme a while to catch my breath and get some circulation back in my hands." She took deep breaths and shook her hands as Dalton massaged her back and legs. "Maybe if I can get that last hole a little bigger, I can step up and get enough reception to call nine-one-one."

Within minutes sensation returned to her hands and she once again ascended the wall. Genn slowly and methodically enlarged another pick mark, her hands blistered and bleeding. *If I just had tape to wrap this shank, this sock's no good.* The chalk fragments fell like light snow on Dalton standing below. An hour passed and then another.

"Please come down and rest, you must be so fatigued."

She was ravenously thirsty. Her tongue stuck to the roof of her mouth. "Let me rest for a while, but I think I'm high enough now to push aside the tin. Then there might be enough reception to call. If there's still not enough signal, I could dial nine-one-one and toss the phone up outta the hole. Maybe then it'll have enough bars for the call to go through. If we yell as loud as we can maybe they'll hear us and get our location. We hafta do something soon. The phone's gonna die."

Her toes struggled to find the lower hole. She shifted her weight and almost slipped. She paused and tried again. This time it felt firm enough. Her fingers found the next hole and then her other toes gripped the little ledge. "I'm slipping, watch out!"

Again he broke her fall and they slumped against the wall. She clung to him and he massaged her cramping legs. "Dehydration is really getting to me." Her voice was almost inaudible.

"Here finish what's left of the water."

"Don't you want some," she offered.

"Oh yes, but you need it more."

Her voice had been little more than a raspy whisper, but the last of the water freed her tongue and made speaking easier. "I could feel some big roots around the edge of the entrance shaft just below the top of the hole. It makes the opening at the surface smaller than the shaft below. That shaft must be about three or so feet across. I'm able to chimney up. Do you know how to do that?"

"I think so, I remember some guys in college who were spelunkers. They used to talk about doing that in a cave in north Alabama and I saw you do it once on the Rec Center climbing wall."

"Just remember to push your back against the wall with your feet and hands. Then move your hands to the wall behind you and push up a few inches. You can get up that way if you're careful and keep applying pressure to the walls."

"That rough surface'll help."

"If I can get a grip on one of those roots, I can pull up far enough to push the tin aside. If I can hold on to the edge of it, I might be able to get out. That would be better than throwing the phone up top."

"What if you looped our belts around one of those roots? If you get out, they might hang far enough down that I could pull myself up. That way those last two holes won't need to be dug out anymore for my big feet." Both wore wide leather belts that if attached might extend four or more feet.

"That might work, take yours off." His was too wide to fit through her belt loops and slide over her belt. Instead she slipped it between her belt and the waistline of her jeans.

Dalton boosted her up. She could feel a burst of adrenalin and this time moved upward with more confidence.

Her blistered and bleeding hands stung as she chimneyed up the entrance shaft and gripped a large exposed root. She pulled herself higher as her feet struggled against the chalk surface. She could feel the corrugations on the underside of the tin and with her fingertips pushed it a few inches aside. Her left hand slipped from the root but her flailing right gripped it firmly. She now hung by both hands. She gritted her teeth as the pain in her fingers and palms neared agony. She pushed against the wall with her feet and again wedged her back against the other side. She reached upwards. Again her fingers pushed against the tin and it moved further.

"Stars! Oh Dalton! I see stars!"

The tin still partially covered the hole. She pushed up and grasped its edge. The corrugations gave the tin enough rigidity to support her. Due to dehydration her weight had slipped below its usual hundred and fifteen pounds, but she was weaker. *This is it. If I can't get out this time we might die down here.*

Her muscles and hands screamed with pain as she grasped the edge of the hole and the root. With her feet scrambling against the rough vertical chalk surface she pulled herself up and felt a gentle night breeze. "I'm out!" she said softly down the hole to Dalton. "Oh thank God, I'm out!"

She sat for a moment in the darkness—her raw hands throbbing. She could feel warm blood beginning to run down her fingers. *Gotta call nine-one-one.*

"Nine-one-one, what's your emergency?" The operator could barely hear a desperate female voice that was breaking up.

"HELP US! My husband's in an old well! We're south of Whitby just off ...." The cellphone screen turned black—a dead battery. *Oh shit! But I'll get him out.*

"Ma'am, where are you?" There was only silence.

30

GENN LAY ON the edge of the cistern opening. In the darkness she could feel one of the roots that was uncovered all the way around. *I can do this! Loop Dalton's belt around that root and pull it back through the buckle.* She slipped it around the root but had to extend her body further to grab the loose end. She almost fell headfirst into the hole but stopped by pushing up with one hand. She pulled the tongue of the belt through the buckle and it tightened. *Now back out carefully.*

"Dalton how can I attach these belts? Knotting them together will take up too much length. You might not be able to reach it."

"What if you lined the holes up and threaded sumthin through? Feel around you, I remember seeing some old 'bob' wire up against that bodock you tied the rope around." His voice sounded distant and muffled.

It was a moonless night. She turned from the hole and gently patted the ground beside her. She felt a mound of soft dirt and then something crawling on her arms. *Fire ants!* They bit almost instantly and she furiously brushed them from her hands and wrists.

"Ouch, damn!"

With her skin still painfully stinging, she found the wire lying in a twisted pile with old fence posts and briars. Three strands extended from the twisted mass to the tree. Slowly over time the trunk had grown over the staples holding the rusty wire in place. On the other side of the tree the wires protruded a foot or so to where they had been cut off many years ago. She grasped one wire with her throbbing right hand and repeatedly flexed it back and forth until she could feel the metal begin to fatigue and break off. *I need another.* She repeated the process.

"Hang on," she yelled hoarsely down the hole. "I'm wiring these belts together."

She overlapped the belt tongues and aligned the two holes nearest the tips. It took little effort to work the wire through and bend back around in a loop. She repeated the process for a second set of holes. "Dalton, I've got them together!"

"Pull on it as hard as you can!"

She grasped the buckle with both hands and pulled back. *It feels solid, but he's a lot heavier.* "It seems strong enough."

"Throw it back down and I'll climb up and grab it." Dalton grasped the first handhold and pulled up, his feet scrambling for the footholds. He gripped the next hole and moved his left hand up to the right and pulled his body high enough to get the tip of his boot into the next.

Gotta get higher. Shifting his weight to his left foot, he reached upwards with his right hand and found the slight ledge. He moved his right foot to the next hole and shifted his weight again. Extending his left arm he was able to grab the ledge and steady himself.

So far so good. He moved his left foot and found another hole.

If I can push up, maybe I can get to the end of that belt! He grabbed in the darkness with his right hand and brushed against the dangling belt buckle. *Now I know where it is.* He paused momentarily to catch his breath. It was hot and damp beneath the crude facemask and the lime dust bitter. He pushed higher and slapped his hand against the wall, pinning the belt.

Almost, almost. He gripped the belt tightly and tested its strength. *Feels okay.* He let go with his left hand and swung his arm as high as he could reach and grabbed the belt just above his right hand. Hand-over-hand he pulled himself up while wedging his back against the wall.

Slowly he inched higher in the hole until he could reach up and grab one of the roots with his right hand. "Genn, I'm going to reach up and grab the edge of the hole with my left hand; then I'm going to reach up out of the hole with my right. Reach down and grasp my wrist with your right."

"Okay, I'm here." She said down into the darkness.

Shifting his weight to his left hand, Dalton reached upwards and tightly grasped her wrist. She in turn firmly gripped his. "Okay, on three, I'm going to push up; you pull as hard as you can."

With the little strength she had left she pulled. He pushed upwards and put his foot on the root and stepped upwards and out of the cistern. For several minutes they lay hyperventilating and embracing on the ground.

"Genn, you're trembling. Your hands and arms are wet, are you bleeding?"

"I'm okay, but it seems that everything in this little part

of the world wants to cut, stab, choke, or bite me," she said with a little laugh as tears trickled down her cheeks leaving unseen tracks in the lime dust.

They painfully rose and he wrapped her hands with the torn pieces of his tee shirt. "I know they're nasty, but that hydrated lime is a good antibiotic. Now, let's get outta here!"

Suddenly behind them a truck engine roared. *Edgar!*

After so many hours in darkness the headlights were blinding. The truck door hinges squeaked loudly as Edgar jumped out pistol in hand. Squinting, Dalton and Genn stood and held each other tightly.

"Well, I'll be damned! Looks like you two figured a way to get out and y'all look and smell like a coupla friggin' zombies. I guess I'll hafta take care of y'all the old fashioned way. Smart boy you're first, but then I'm gonna have some real fun wallowin' around on top of yo skinny little bitch! Course she won't enjoy it very much!"

"You bastard!" cried Dalton as he started towards Edgar.

In one fluid motion, Genn pulled the shank from her hip pocket and lunged with her body and arm extended— her full weight behind it. The pistol fired as Genn made contact knocking him off balance. As he staggered, Genn could feel the shank sink into the side of his throat just below his jaw. Screaming, she pushed with all her strength and twisted the blade from side to side. She kneed Edgar in the groin repeatedly and struggled to grab the hand holding the pistol. It fired again but into the ground. She felt warm liquid spewing on her arms and shirt. Edgar struggled less and less as his throat gurgled. Genn snatched the pistol and grasped it with both hands. She stood over him and fired again and again into his torso. Edgar's body jerked obscenely in a Dance Macabre. Even after the last shell casing ejected and the slide locked open, she continued pulling the trigger. She fell upon him, savagely smashing the butt of the pistol into his face.

"Dalton, Dalton, are you okay?" He lay clutching his left side. The bullet had pierced a lung and exited at an angle. It continued on through his left arm shattering the bone just above his elbow. Arterial blood pulsed from the wound. Genn pulled off her already bloody shirt, quickly folded it into a compress, and applied pressure.

"Oh this hurts so bad," moaned Dalton through his clenched teeth. "Genn, never forget how much I love you."

"Yeah, yeah, don't be melodramatic. You're gonna be okay, just hang in there, don't pass out. Edgar's not a problem anymore." It suddenly occurred to her that they were alone in the middle of a pasture nearly a half-mile from the highway.

Crickets, distant spring peepers, and Dalton's soft groaning provided the only sounds. She knelt beside him holding the compress on his arm. Fortunately the entrance and exit wounds on his left side bled slowly, but when Dalton breathed, air wheezed in and out of both holes. *Dear Lord, please don't let him die.*

Few motorists drove Highway 95 at night. Only occasionally did she see headlights. In vain she screamed for help knowing she couldn't be heard. Dalton's respiration was becoming irregular. Genn struggled against panic. *Stay calm,* she thought. *Keep him conscious! Keep up the pressure!*

Edgar's pickup sat a few feet away—its lights still on. Options swirled in the fog of her mind. *The keys, where are the keys? Are they in the ignition or did Edgar take them out, would the truck even start? I would have to get him up, but he's too weak to stand. I'm too weak to drag him and hold this compress.*

A tourniquet, get a tourniquet on his arm! But there's no way to find something to use without him losing more blood! Can't use our belts, they're in the hole and I can't get them without letting go of the compress. My bra, but it'd take two hands to get it off. He's too weak to hold it in place himself! If I got him in the truck, what about the gate? It's probably locked—what if I drove through it—but the truck might stall or get stuck.

"Stay awake, Dalton! Stay awake! I know you're tired but please stay awake." She cried hoarsely. *Oh God help us!*

"Where are we, Dalton?"

"Edgar's place."

"Where do we work?"

"University."

"What's my sister's name?"

"Lillian," he said with a faint smile.

"What color are my eyes?"

"Green."

"Look into them Dalton! I love you with all my heart."

"Oh Genn," he whispered softly through blistered lips.

"Keep your eyes open!" But Dalton's eyes began to roll back and his eyelids fluttered. "Dalton! Dalton!" Tears began rolling down her cheeks. "Pray with me," she hoarsely whispered, "Our Father which art in Heaven, hallowed be Thy Name. Thy Kingdom come, Thy will be done …."

The sounds of the night suddenly seemed a little different. There was a faint high-pitched wail in the distance. It grew louder and suddenly she could see flashing red and blue lights on Highway 95. Two vehicles stopped at the gate. A horn blared and over a speaker came a voice, "Genn, Dalton are y'all out there?"

Genn tried to speak but her voice sounded like a throttled frog. She half-raised her body and waved with one hand. From the gate came a spotlight beam that swept back and forth across them. The light almost blinded her, but she kept waving frantically.

From across the field she heard a voice. "Forget the damn lock—follow me!"

An engine raced and with a crash the patrol car smashed through. Dragging the gate and long strands of barbed wire with uprooted fence posts still attached, it sped down the field road and across the browse line. Lucius jumped out and ran to Genn and Dalton.

"He's dying, help me!"

"Let the EMTs take over—a helicopter's on the way. We'll get him to Tuscaloosa."

"This one's in shock, he's lost consciousness. Get that IV started!"

"Oh Dalton, don't die!"

"We're doing our best ma'am, let us do our job."

Lucius gently blotted her mouth and face with gauze and gave her sips of water. One of the EMTs cocooned her hands in bandages, covered her with a blanket, and slid her onto an emergency stretcher. Numb with exhaustion Genn didn't feel the insertion of an IV needle.

"Where's Dalton?" she murmured.

"He's on this other stretcher ma'am. He unconscious but I think he'll begin to stabilize with the IV and oxygen."

"How did you know?" she whispered to Lucius.

"Your nine-one-one call got through. The operator heard your voice for just a moment before the phone went dead. Caller ID told her it was Dalton's phone. The cellular company triangulated your position, but it took nearly an hour. I knew we had to get here fast."

"Won't the boss be mad when he sees your patrol car?" she said softly with a faint smile.

"Believe me; his only concern will be that y'all made it."

Her body shook as she softly wept. "But we might lose Dalton."

"It'll be okay, it'll be okay." Lucius said with his hand on her shoulder as the EMTs immobilized her on the stretcher.

In the distance aircraft lights flickered just above the treetops and the thump of rotors grew louder and louder. All around them dust and debris swirled. Genn could feel her stretcher being lifted into the helicopter and fastened down. The whine of the helicopter's turbine as it lifted off faded in her ears as painless darkness engulfed her.

31

CONFUSION, MUFFLED VOICES, blessed unconsciousness. Intermittent dreams of childhood. Running. Running from pursuers. Running from Edgar. Dalton's face and a gentle kiss. She partially opened her eyes but her eyelids were sticky. Two faces loomed but she couldn't focus.

"Dalton's alive and getting better," said a familiar voice. "More rest and you'll be okay."

"Pop, Lillian," she tried to say with an indistinct rasp.

"Don't speak. Your mouth, throat, and eyes are burned from breathing all that lime dust. Her father put a pen in her hand, "Try writing."

Her swollen fingers could not grasp the pen so she held it like a dagger and scrawled on the tablet held by her sister, "Dalton where?"

"You're both in Druid City Hospital. Dalton's in Intensive Care, he's improving and has to have surgery on his arm. The doctor got his lung re-inflated."

"Edgar?" she wrote.

"He's dead," said her father. "You saved Dalton's life and your own."

Tears welled in her eyes.

"Sis, you did what you had to do."

"How long?" she scratched on the tablet.

"You've been asleep for over sixty hours," said a nurse joining them at bedside. "Your mouth and throat should heal quickly, maybe in a day or two you'll be able to speak a little better and begin a regular diet. Your vision should rapidly improve. Your sister mentioned an extra pair of glasses in your office at the University that someone is bringing."

"Your other pair was broken in the fight with Edgar," interjected Lillian.

"We removed the bandages from your hands a few hours ago. I know those injuries were painful, but actually they're superficial. We need to get you out of bed and walking."

"See Dalton," she wrote tearing the top sheet on the pad.

"We can do that Dr. Randolph, but first let's get you up and walking a few steps around the room. Then we'll get you in a wheelchair and go down to Intensive Care."

She was stiff and incredibly sore, but with assistance from the nurse and her sister she haltingly limped across the room. "Let's take a few more steps and then sit in this wheelchair."

Genn sat and gestured as if brushing her hair. "I'll brush it," said Lillian. "I know how much Dalton loves your hair."

She brushed Genn's hair gently to avoid pulling the many tangles. After a few dozen strokes, Genn nodded and pointed towards the door.

"Dr. Randolph, we'll go to the ICU, but your husband probably isn't conscious and if he is he may not be able to respond. His physicians are optimistic that he'll recover."

The Intensive Care rooms were crowded with

instruments and medical devices. Dalton lay prone attached to various tubes and wires. Overhead, a monitor constantly displayed his vital signs.

As Lillian pushed her sister's wheelchair to the room, one of the physicians approached. "Mrs. Randolph, it's so good to see you up and about. I'm Dr. Ritchfield. You husband is quite a strong man. His vital signs look excellent today. We're increasingly optimistic he'll make a good recovery. Fortunately we were able to save his left arm but he'll need multiple surgeries. His lung should be okay, the bullet's initial entry went between two ribs but when it exited a rib was broken. The lung should be okay with no permanent impairment."

Genn reached out and covered his right hand with hers. *Dear God, thank You for sparing his life.*

"Dr. Randolph, we're limited to five-minute visits in ICU. We'll step outside and leave you alone with your husband for now," said the nurse.

"Mr. Hastings, your daughter is one of the bravest people I've ever known," said Dr. Ritchfield. "Plus you may not know this since y'all have been here for nearly three days but she has become quite a celebrity. Her story's all over the national media and has even been picked up by the BBC and other world news services. There are even two newborns in our Women's Center that have been named for her."

Since losing consciousness Dalton floated in darkness. Time was meaningless. Nights and days passed. Gradually he became aware of light and sound—lights overhead and the sounds of medical equipment. Occasionally the lights flickered as if clouds passed over him. Gradually he began to feel pain—his arm and back aching miserably.

"Do you hurt?"

"Uhhh," he groaned with a slight nod. In moments the pain faded and he drifted back into blackness. Hours passed and the light returned.

"Dr. Randolph, you can hear me can't you?"

He licked his lips and mouthed, "Yes."

"Good, we're cutting back on the pain meds. You should begin to stay conscious longer."

He felt something warm grasp his hand. "Dalton, we're alive. Everything is going to be okay."

"Genn, Genn," he tried to whisper.

"Don't talk ... just know that I'm with you."

She sat silently holding his hand for the rest of the visitation period. When the nurse touched her shoulder and whispered it was time to go, Dalton gently squeezed her hand. She knew then they would survive.

Three days passed. Genn's vision improved and with her spare bifocals she began reading newspaper accounts of their disappearance and ordeal. One of her graduate students had even recorded television news stories and replayed them for her. By now cards and flowers filled her room. She had just finished a chapter of *Tuscaloosa Moon*, a novel written by one of her friends several years ago, when someone softly rapped on the partially open door.

"Good afternoon, Mrs. Randolph. We're with the Vestavia Hills Police Department. This is Detective Reardon and I'm Detective Maddingley. You and your husband have been through quite an ordeal. We hope you're feeling better and that your husband is mending. If you could spare us a few minutes, we would appreciate it very much."

"Certainly Detectives, I'm feeling much better and Dalton may be out of intensive care later today. Hopefully I can go home in a couple of days. But I do tire rather easily and you'll have to listen to my raspy voice. What can I do for you?"

"We're investigating the disappearance of Belinda Dunstan, you may have heard about her being missing," said Maddingley.

"I do remember seeing some news stories about it before Dalton and I got involved in our little 'adventure.'"

"When you and your husband were confined in that cistern did y'all see or hear anything that might relate to her?"

"Something I clearly recall about the bodies down there is that one of the most recent, that is to say near the top of the pile, is a woman in what appeared to be a nice cocktail dress."

"Can you describe her?"

"Her features were bloated and she was covered with lime dust. But I would say she was middle-aged with a slender build. Her hair may have been blond, but there was so much dust."

"What about the dress?" asked Reardon.

"It may have been a dark color, perhaps black. It looked rather expensive like a Halston design. But haven't the bodies been removed yet?"

"That's gonna be quite an undertaking and may take several weeks. The FBI lowered someone down there for a preliminary look but there're ventilation and lighting issues that'll make evidence gathering very difficult under the current circumstances. Forensic scientists and archaeologists will need to be in there for quite a while. I believe they're gonna excavate an access tunnel from the side of the hill."

"Did you notice anything else about the bodies?" asked Maddingley.

"Several were wearing braids or weaves. They might have been young African American males. Oh yeah, something else about the woman, she wasn't wearing jewelry or a watch. I distinctly remember that, since we thought if she had a watch, it might still be working. Being down there with almost no light was very disorienting and our cell phone battery was low."

"Did Wellton ever give you any indication of what was going on?"

"I kept trying to convince him to let us go. I told him that we didn't think he had killed any of those people and perhaps if he cooperated he might get probation and be put in a witness protection program, maybe out West."

"How did he react to that suggestion?"

"I really thought he was considering it since he tossed us a bottle of water, but he said his 'friends' were everywhere and that there was 'no place to hide.'"

"Did he say anything else about his 'friends?'" asked Maddingley. "Who they might be?"

"Only that they were all over the place."

"Any other questions for now, Peggy?"

Reardon shook her head.

"Thank you for talking with us. We may have more questions later. Here are our cards, if you remember anything else call us at any time."

Reardon and Maddingley's car merged into traffic on McFarland Boulevard as they headed for the Interstate 20/59 interchange. "I think we have enough now to get a warrant for the 'good doctor.' With his money he could bolt at any time, so hopefully the judge won't allow bail."

"Agreed," nodded Maddingley. "I'll phone in and start the ball rolling. Maybe we'll have that warrant this afternoon."

32

THE SPARTAN INTERVIEW room contained a simple metal table and four chairs. Daniel Dunstan and his attorney, Cyrus Sunderford, sat on one side.

"Okay Dunstan, we need to talk," said Reardon as she and her partner entered the room.

"Before we begin, how about removing these handcuffs from my client? They're obviously uncomfortable and for a man of his stature in this community, it's humiliating."

"We can do that," said Maddingley retrieving keys from his pocket. "Y'all need water, coffee, or a soft drink?" Both shook their head.

"Have you found my wife?" asked Dunstan.

"Yes," said Reardon, "we believe so. First of all, we have a body that appears to be your wife's. However, final identification is pending. Evidence has to be collected and the remains removed from a site that is difficult to access. At this point the FBI has control of that area."

"You're saying my wife is dead," said Dunstan, as he lowered his head into his hands.

"So you're *alleging* this to be the body of my client's wife."

"Based upon our preliminary investigation we believe with some certainty that it is her," averred Maddingley.

"I did not kill my wife! Yes, she had problems, but I loved her very much!"

"Dunstan," stated Reardon, "I'm going to do something out of the ordinary during an investigation. I'm going to reveal to you and your attorney some of our evidence so you can understand what you're up against."

Sunderford straightened up in his chair and stared intently at Reardon with considerable suspicion. "And why would you do that?"

"It's very simple," said Maddingley. "We want truthful answers from you and justice for the victims."

Reardon looked Dunstan in the eye. "We've got witnesses who saw you leave the party with your wife and this is verified by the parking deck's security video. Your own security system video shows you and someone resembling your wife return to your mansion later that evening. Then, the next afternoon, that person left in your wife's car. But that person *was not your wife*. She was a young woman named Kicky Harris, a waitress from Walker County. We know who she was because part of a tattoo of her name was visible behind her ear. She did not wear your wife's scarf low enough to cover it. Two days later she died in a suspicious house trailer fire that appears to be arson. The video shows that when Kicky Harris left your home, she was wearing your wife's Harry Winston engagement ring. That's the ring in the photo we showed you earlier. A firefighter took that ring after finding it hidden in the sofa that Kicky Harris died on. That firefighter sold that ring to a pawnbroker who tried to have it smuggled out of the country," stated Reardon.

"I repeat! I did not kill my wife! I have no idea who this Kicky Harris is or how she got my wife's ring!"

"It's best not to say anything else," cautioned Cyrus Sunderford.

Detective Reardon rose from her chair, leaned forward, and pointed at Dunstan. "You obviously had accomplices in arranging your wife's death. I want to read something. Your attorney, of course, is quite familiar with it. This is from the Code of Alabama, Title 13A, that's the Criminal Code. The following is one of the capital offenses, 'Murder done for a pecuniary or other valuable consideration or pursuant to a contract or for hire.' A capital offense means the death penalty. If convicted, you *will be* sentenced to death by lethal injection. The evidence against you is substantial and much more is forthcoming."

"With all due respect Detective, aren't you getting a little melodramatic? Let's take a break so I can confer with my client in private?"

"Yes of course," said Maddingley. "There, the recording system's off. We'll be outside, let us know when we can return."

"Whew," said Reardon. "That felt good. I haven't had the opportunity to forcefully interrogate a suspect in a long time!"

The hall door opened and a casually dressed figure approached them. "Mornin' Detectives," said Mayor Covingdon. "I heard about the arrest and wanted to know if I could chat with y'all for a few moments in private?"

"Sure Mayor," said Maddingley. "Let's use this other interview room. We're taking a break while Dunstan and his lawyer confer."

Reardon closed the door behind them. "What's up?" asked Reardon.

"Well, I don't want you to think I'm interfering but I've been talkin' to some of our business leaders and realty folks. They're really concerned about this Dunstan thing."

"In what way, sir?" asked Maddingley.

"The main concern for everyone, including me, is that this case will create a lot more adverse publicity for our city. But let me ask you this, strictly off the record, how does the evidence against him look?"

"Very, very solid, I'd say that so far we have some of the strongest circumstantial evidence I've ever seen in a murder case," said Reardon with emphasis. "It's murder for hire almost certainly and that is a capital offense."

Mayor Covingdon nodded grimly. "The District Attorney told me earlier that a sentence of life without parole is possible, especially if the defendant confesses and cooperates. Dunstan may have hired some group, a gang so to speak, that keeps an extremely low profile. The FBI is anxious to learn more about them. If you get him to confess, a plea bargain is possible. That way the case can be concluded quickly. If it goes to trial and he gets a death sentence, this thing could drag on for decades. And quite frankly our city does not need that sorta publicity."

"And that would be bad for business," interjected Maddingley with a roll of his eyes.

"It would be bad for the entire community, Detective! We are now the third largest city in Jefferson County. Our real estate values are solid, our schools some of the very best, and our crime rate low. And we mean to keep it that way. The best thing that can happen is that Dunstan is convicted and sent away for good. In time most people will forget about it and there won't be news stories constantly reminding everyone over and over again for the next twenty-five years that he's on Death Row."

"Mayor, we'll keep working on him. After all, what we want is for the truth to come out. Belinda Dunstan and Kicky Harris may not have seemed to be very sympathetic characters to some folks but they deserve justice," said Reardon.

"Thanks Detectives, I'll let you get back to work," said Covingdon as he left.

"Peggy, what do you think?"

"I'd like to see the damned bastard strapped down on that execution gurney at Atmore. After all he's responsible for the deaths of two women. But I can't let personal feelings get in the way. I say we just need to do our jobs. If the DA wants to plea bargain and Dunstan can provide information that will help with a larger investigation, then it's fine by me."

"Well, time for me to make a solo appearance—looks like they're through with their little confab."

"You guys through conferring?" asked Maddingley as he opened the interview room door.

"We're finished," said Sunderford.

"I hafta apologize for Detective Reardon. She gets worked up sometimes and can be rather intense."

"So you're the 'good cop,'" said Sunderford with a condescending hand gesture.

"All of us try to be good cops," Maddingley said thoughtfully as he sat directly across from Dunstan. "I want what is best for everyone, but especially for Belinda

Dunstan and Kicky Harris. I want the truth and justice, not vengeance."

"And what do you believe to be the truth?" asked Dunstan.

"That you paid someone or some group to kill your wife for some reason or reasons known only to you. And that in the process Kicky Harris was also murdered."

"I did not pay to have my wife killed and I've never heard of this ... Kicky Harris."

"Dunstan, we have overwhelming evidence that you did and that the process resulted in the death of Kicky Harris, your wife's double. Now we can go on for days or even weeks like this questioning you every day. But every day the evidence will only get stronger, especially when we recover your wife's body and do a thorough forensics analysis. Detective Reardon may have been rather forceful but she is one-hundred-percent correct. Murder for hire in Alabama is a capital offense. However, depending upon the circumstances, especially if the accused confesses and cooperates, a reduction of the sentence to life without parole is possible."

"I can't confess to something I didn't do."

"Look at it this way. You could spend the rest of your life filing endless appeals for a stay of execution or retrial and then have your life terminated lying on that awful white gurney. Or you can be in prison without the death penalty hanging over your head and you can put your talents to good use. In that initial interview just after you reported your wife missing, you expressed deep satisfaction at helping people in that free clinic—the poor, the homeless, the mentally ill. You could work in the prison's clinic or hospital, not as a physician of course, but as someone whose knowledge and compassion would help others."

Dunstan stared at the tabletop. "I didn't have her killed."

"You can spare yourself a lot of grief and pain plus save your life by confessing. The DA's office may be willing to enter a plea bargain agreement if you cooperate with us and the FBI. You could avoid a lengthy and humiliating trial and years or even decades of uncertainty on Death Row. I want you to sincerely think about it. Not only would your life be spared but others could still benefit from your skills and your wife and that poor waitress from Walker County would have justice. That's the best possible outcome for everyone. Talk it over with your attorney and consider what I've said. We'll talk more later."

Maddingley walked down the hall to his cubicle. "Looks like you need this," said Reardon handing him a bottle of water. "Good Lord, Clayton after that you've got ME ready to confess. Let's call it a day and go home."

As they walked down the hall Chief Haskell patted Maddingley on the back. "You and Reardon are doing a good job on this case."

33

THE MASSIVE EXCAVATOR roared to life as its smoky exhaust rose from behind the hillside. "I didn't know rock could be excavated without blasting," said Agent Delbert Hulditch of the Birmingham FBI office as he, Sheriff Mosby, and Deputy Jones overlooked the site.

"We do it every day of the week at the quarry," said Millar Nettleton as he approached the group. "That bucket has special ripper teeth that'll cut right through this chalk. Come on down and see it in action. Here, put on these hardhats and stay back from either side of the excavator. The operator'll be emptyin' that bucket into dump trucks that'll come up alongside. They'll spoil that material away from the trench. I wouldn't mind hauling that stuff back to the plant. It looks like good feedstock for the cement kiln. But we can't since we'd hafta have a mining permit for this site and of course the owner is deceased."

An engineer had chosen a starting point about two hundred feet downhill from the cistern. The design called for a trench extending into the hillside and ending with a vertical wall about twenty feet high. From there an entrance tunnel would penetrate into the cistern.

"It won't take long to excavate the trench. We just have to keep a check on the grade to make sure it drains back away from the cistern. We don't want a sudden thunderstorm flooding it out."

"How much chalk do y'all hafta remove?" asked Mosby.

"About fifteen-hundred cubic yards—that's about two thousand tons—if we don't hafta slope the sides back very much."

"That sounds like a lot," interjected Hulditch.

"Well, a lot of days at the quarry we'll take out several times that much. That kiln has a big appetite."

"How long?" asked Sheriff Mosby.

"We may finish tomorrow and then we can dig the access tunnel."

"By hand?"

"In a way," Nettleton laughed. "Believe it or not we're gonna cut it out with a special chainsaw—won't take but a few hours. Then we're gonna mount a steel security door in the opening. The men'll push it in place and shoot in some rock bolts to secure the frame. That door has a stout deadbolt so y'all can lock 'er up good and tight when nobody's in there."

"Any risk of it fallin' in?" asked Deputy Jones.

"Chalk's usually pretty stable. But sometimes it has cracks so that it might not stay together after we cut through and we don't wanna take any chances. We're gonna line the tunnel with heavy wire mesh to prevent rock falls. We hafta go by all the Federal mining regs."

"This is a first time experience for me," said Hulditch shaking his head in disbelief.

The crew from the quarry continued working the rest

of the day and through the night with the assistance of generator-powered floodlights. By the next morning the trench stretched into the hillside and stopped with less than ten feet of chalk remaining before the interior of the cistern would be breached. A pickup backed into the trench and two workmen removed a security door and its frame and stood it against the wall at the end of the trench. They marked the outline of the frame with spray paint.

"Now we're getting close," said Nettleton as one of the workmen started a chain saw and began cutting into the chalk along the painted outline. Within minutes a cut had been incised nearly a foot and a half into the rock face.

"What Dalton and Genn would have given for that chainsaw when they were in that cistern," said Lucius.

"There're all kinda saws for cutting into rock, some of 'em real monsters. This one's probably best suited for what we're doing since one man can handle it."

The workman angled his next cuts and a helper began removing chunks of the soft chalk. Within several hours they penetrated to within a foot or so of the cistern. The security door was set into place and the frame attached with rock bolts and the heavy mesh lining mounted. Wearing respirators the workmen removed the final relatively thin wall of chalk separating the cistern from the tunnel. They cleared the remaining debris and closed the security door.

"All right! Time to get this show on the road," said Hulditch as one of the workmen tossed him the keys. He walked the length of the trench, unlocked, and opened the steel door. The stench overwhelmed him as air rushed out. Hulditch turned and walked away quickly to avoid vomiting. "Start the air!" he yelled as he gagged.

On top of the little hill a switch was thrown. A ventilation fan began sucking air from the top of the cistern while fresh air rushed in through the newly installed door. "Let's give it a few minutes to get some of the foul air and lime dust out," said Nettleton.

"Go ahead and turn on the lights," shouted Hulditch. A suspended cluster of floodlights that had been lowered in the hole at the top were switched on.

Wearing a safety mask and hardhat Hulditch cautiously stepped through the door and approached the point the tunnel opened into the cistern. Dust still lingered but he could feel fresh air rushing in around him. Although light filtered down from above, he still needed a large LED flashlight to clearly make out what lay before him. It looked as if snow had fallen and blanketed the interior of the cistern but there were footprints everywhere left by the Randolphs.

"God Almighty, how did they survive in here?" he said softly as his eyes followed the path of their foot and handholds extending diagonally across the wall. Opposite where he stood lay a pile of lumpy white shapes—corpses.

"Sir, please don't go any further," said a forensics technician standing behind him. "We have to take detailed photos before anything is disturbed."

"Oh, sure," said Hulditch obviously stunned by the scene that lay before him. He backed out and stood beside Sheriff Mosby. "I can't believe what I just saw."

Mosby slowly shook his head, "Me neither. Your technical folks are gonna be here a long time."

As the trio walked away, Mardi Tilden glanced at a fellow technician, "Looks like we'll be stuck in that roach motel in Whitby for a few weeks, unless we can find a place in Tuscaloosa that'll accept government rate."

"Yeah or we could stay onsite in that old trailer over there," said Johanna Symington with a snicker, "Bathe in a rain barrel and walk to work every morning. But hey, we'd be saving a big chunk of our per diem."

"Why do I always get a smartass for a roommate?" pleaded Mardi looking up at the overcast sky.

"Just hush up and check the cameras, we've got lots of pictures to take."

34

DETECTIVES REARDON AND Maddingley entered the room. Daniel Dunstan and Cyrus Sunderford sat side-by-side at a table.

"Mornin' Dunstan, Counselor," said Maddingley with a nod. "Have you discussed and considered what we told you three days ago?"

"Yes, but my client still maintains his innocence."

"As we previously stated, more and more evidence comes in daily. The FBI forensic people have been able to access that cistern down in Tombigbee County. They've examined the body of a woman that lay on top of that pile of corpses. The dress she wore is an exact duplicate of the one left by Kicky Harris in your wife's bedroom. We now have proof you bought two identical Halston dresses—one for your wife and the other for her double. Your wife's dental records have been checked against that body. Dunstan, that's your wife they found down there in that hole and it's obvious she was murdered."

Dunstan lowered his head into his hands and sobbed. "Oh God forgive me! I did it."

"Detectives, my client is ready to make a statement and we'd like to meet later with someone from the DA's office."

—⁓—

Agent Hulditch stared across the table at Dunstan. He had interviewed murderers before—drug cartel members, street thugs, cold socio-paths, Middle Eastern terrorists, racial supremacists, and war criminals. But never had he faced a wealthy and respected physician. In his orange jumpsuit, Dunstan looked plain and small—nondescript. *He doesn't seem capable of murder.*

"Dunstan, I've reviewed your statement to the police and DA. We're going to go over everything. I have a number of questions."

"I've already revealed everything I know," he said softly.

"We need to make sure of the details, plus the Bureau takes a wider, or rather, national view of things."

"Okay," he said with a halting nod.

"Why did you want your wife dead?"

Dunstan sighed deeply. "I worked so hard for decades to achieve my goals—a respected career, social status, wealth. I thought those things would make Belinda happy. But she hated our lifestyle. She missed her late family from Lawrence County and of course we never had children. She felt socially inferior and never thought herself worthy of our position. So she drank constantly when it came time for most social events, which was quite often. Years ago I started prescribing anti-anxiety meds but those didn't help."

"So she became a liability?"

"I began to feel that way. I just couldn't understand her behavior. She had a great sense of style, always dressed appropriately, and had a small circle of close friends. But she couldn't handle public situations with casual acquaintances or strangers. The only thing that seemed to give her pleasure was nice jewelry. Her heart seemed to be in that built-in jewelry cabinet in her room. Then I met Amelia." He paused and looked down at his hands.

"Tell me about Amelia."

"She was just a shop girl when I met her. She worked the counter at Mendelssohn's. I went there to buy something for Belinda's birthday. Amelia was helpful and insightful about what to purchase since she had assisted Belinda several times before. I went by other times and got to know her. In many ways she was like Belinda, attractive, well-spoken, elegant, and from a rural background. Her family lived just above poverty but like me she wanted fine things—and respect. We met several times for lunch at a little café near her shop. We became lovers."

"How did she become your wife's social secretary or personal assistant?"

"That was easy. Belinda just couldn't handle all the details. You know keeping track of her calendar, writing thank you notes, taking care of her jewelry and clothes. Basically just managing her life."

"Was there any one event that triggered your decision to have her killed?"

"It had been on my mind for quite some time. But the scene at the Art Museum when she threw that seventy-five thousand dollar vase at me was the last straw. It was humiliating. I felt then that she had to go."

"Why not just divorce her?"

"That would have been messy—very messy indeed. I had approached her about it before but the very mention sent her into a rage. She vowed she would destroy me if I ever tried."

"Did she suspect your relationship with Amelia Baker?"

"I don't think she had any idea."

"In reading your statement to the police and prosecutor, I got the impression you were intentionally misleading them as to how you arranged her death."

"There's really nothing to elaborate on. A security guard who worked at our clinic made the arrangements. And as I said before, I never saw him again after they took Belinda the night of the engagement party."

"Dunstan, I have a hard time believing that. This whole scheme was far, far too elaborate and had to involve a number of people. Let me tell you what happened. First we know you're trying to protect Amelia Baker."

"She had nothing to do with it."

"Oh, yes she did. She's in this as deep as you are. Her brother from over in Mississippi was imprisoned several years ago at Parchman Farm. There he joined a secretive gang. He and his cohorts came to know Edgar Wellton and learned of his land and that old cistern in Tombigbee County. The decision was made to recruit Wellton as an associate and use his land and cistern as a disposal site for victims of contract killings after his release. We found bodies in addition to your wife's from all over the Southeast—Atlanta, Nashville, New Orleans, and other cities. Amelia Baker arranged for your wife's murder at your request."

Dunstan stared silently at Hulditch.

"How much, how much did you pay to have your wife murdered?"

"Two hundred thousand dollars."

"How did you make payment?"

"Two cash payments. Amelia gave her brother fifty thousand as a down payment and when they took Belinda after the party I gave them another one hundred fifty thousand in a large envelope—one-hundred dollar bills, fifteen hundred of them."

"How did you get a hold of so much cash?"

"It wasn't difficult. I have accounts in a number of banks. I already kept quite a bit of cash in safety deposit boxes as an emergency fund. Amelia and I would withdraw a few thousand at a time from each account over several months and we stockpiled it in the garage. We only went to the safety deposit boxes once to keep from arousing suspicion."

"How were the arrangements made?"

"It was all written down. Amelia would meet her brother in Tuscaloosa. That way there were no emails, regular mail, or phone calls. She destroyed all the papers after we read them. I never met her brother."

"Did you have contact with anyone else?"

"Only the night it happened and I never saw their faces. There was the security guard at the door as we left that I signaled."

"Well, we're still checking on him."

"Have you arrested Amelia's brother?"

"Let's just say that Mr. Benjamin Maurice Baker met with an accident."

"Accident?"

"Yeah, he fell from the tenth floor of a New Orleans Hotel. The NOPD and coroner ruled it to be a suicide."

"What about the guy from Atlanta who was in the newspapers—the one with a body in the back of his truck?"

"He was out on bond, but if you can't swim you should stay outta the Chattahoochee River."

35

FOUR PEOPLE STOOD under a partly cloudy sky on a breezy late spring day. In front of them lay an open grave containing a simple wooden coffin.

"He led a troubled life," concluded Reverend Victoria Littleberry, "and caused pain for many. But God loves him just as He loves us all."

As a benediction Reverend Littleberry and the others linked hands and recited the Lord's Prayer. The group walked slowly from the cemetery. Sheriff Mosby pardoned himself and left in his patrol car. Deputy Lucius Jones hugged Genn as he started to leave. "Tell Dalton I'll come up to see him tomorrow evening," he said as he got into his truck.

"Vicky, I can't help but have doubts about what I did," said Genn. "I just wish there had been some way to have avoided killing Edgar."

"Sometimes we have to make decisions that involve preservation of our loved ones and ourselves. You did what Edgar and the circumstances compelled you to do. The taking of a life is something none of us would ever want to be forced to do. Do not doubt for a moment that you did the right thing. Pray for Edgar but put him and what he did behind you."

Genn walked to her car and drove away to be with Dalton at the hospital in Tuscaloosa. Behind her, an elderly black man cranked a small rusty backhoe and began filling the grave in the far corner of the Coleman's Corner United Methodist Church Cemetery. High overhead several vultures soared on rising air currents.

—m—

"When did your relationship with Dunstan begin?" asked Agent Hulditch.

"In about 2004, back when I was with Mendelssohn's ... I was very young."

"How did it start?"

"We met when he came in to inquire about a belated engagement ring for his wife. We talked about what sort of ring she might like. After some research I called him a few days later with information about a Sotheby's auction that included several nice rings. He wanted to meet for lunch to review some photos of them. He told me how much he loved Belinda but that she had an alcohol problem and he suspected her of being unfaithful. I guess I started falling for him then. I felt sorry for him, he was so nice."

"What happened after that?"

"Mrs. Mendelssohn liked the work I had been doing and sent me to New York to attend the auction. We could have bid by phone but she wanted me to get some experience. I was able to buy the ring he particularly liked at a price within his budget and brought it back. We went out to lunch after he picked it up. Later we continued to meet and eventually became lovers."

"How did you become Belinda Dunstan's personal assistant?"

"Over the years Belinda's behavior became more and more erratic. She would forget important dates—social events, appointments—other things like that. Plus she often misplaced expensive jewelry. Dan suggested that she needed a personal assistant or social secretary. And he suggested that I would be quite capable of helping her."

"So you moved in?"

"Yes, we wanted to be married but Belinda refused a divorce."

"Did she know about your relationship with her husband?"

"No, I don't think she even suspected it."

"Was there any particular event that triggered the decision to kill her?"

"Her behavior had become an embarrassment and a source of constant gossip in their social circle. She went into rehab several times, but always relapsed. Then one evening about two years ago, Dan said he wished she would die. Nothing came of it at the time but a few months later she caused a scene at their club and was sick all over the dining room carpet before she passed out. One of the waiters helped Dan load her in the car so he could get her home. We cleaned her up and put her to bed. Dan was in tears later that night when I tried to console him. Again he said it would be best if she were dead. But I think the scene at the museum pushed him over the edge."

"And what happened then?"

"I told him that maybe I could make arrangements. Someone I knew once bragged that if anyone needed to disappear he could handle it."

"And who was that?"

"Just a casual acquaintance I met at a party several years ago. He introduced himself as 'Joe.' I never knew his real name and only saw him a few times. I got back in touch with him through a mutual friend—the one who gave the party. We agreed to communicate by handwritten notes instead of phones, email, or regular mail. We would meet in a shopping center parking lot in Hoover."

"Do you still have any of those notes?"

"You should know, the police searched my little apartment and went through all my personal belongings. To answer your question, I flushed the notes after reading them."

"Are you sure you don't know this person's name?"

"Absolutely."

"I have to disclose that we know who it is."

"Okay, who is it?"

"Your brother—Benjamin Baker."

"You're saying my brother is involved in this? That's crazy, you're fishing."

"Oh, it's quite simple. He was in prison in Mississippi, Parchman Farm, at the same time as Edgar Wellton, the man who hid bodies in that cistern down in Tombigbee County. Your brother and Wellton became involved with a criminal organization, a gang. After they were paroled both remained affiliated. Your brother went to Walker County where he moved in with his old college girlfriend, Kicky Harris."

"I've never heard of her."

"You didn't know her name, but you know who she was. She was Belinda Dunstan's double. Kicky died in a house trailer fire a few days after Belinda's disappearance."

"But he couldn't have been involved ... he could never have killed his girlfriend."

"Oh, but he did. We found his DNA on the cigarette that started the fire that killed Kicky."

"Where did you get his DNA to compare it to?"

"The New Orleans Police shared it with us."

"He's in jail in New Orleans?"

"I'm sorry to have to tell you, he's in the Orleans Parish Morgue. He *fell* from a hotel window a few weeks ago."

"Oh my God," she exclaimed putting her hands to her mouth, "Ben's dead!"

"Agent Hulditch, I protest," said her attorney, "this is cruel beyond description!"

"No, counselor, not as cruel as the deaths of Belinda Dunstan and Kicky Harris."

36

"HEY DALTON, THIS is Lucius. Sherwyn's with me on a speaker phone. How're your arm and ribs?"

"It's been a rough six months. The ribs have knitted, but I'm still sore. The arm needs more work but the surgeon says that after this last procedure and more rehab it'll be almost back to normal."

"Put us on your speaker phone if Genn's there. We've got news," said Sherwyn.

"I wanted to clue you in before the press conference," said Lucius. "We're finally getting some resolution. The FBI lab has been able to identify all twenty-three sets of remains through DNA comparisons with relatives. We've cleared at least twenty-two missing person cases and hopefully as many murders."

"That's great, but what about number twenty-three?" asked Genn.

"Well, that's where the case gets *strange*. We asked Sherwyn to consult confidentially. I'm gonna let him tell you about it."

"I checked out the physical evidence for number twenty-three—not the bones but stuff like buttons and buckles.

There's even a voodoo amulet—an 1834 quarter with a skull carved over the figure on the front. I think it might be some sort of curse. All those things date back to the early nineteenth century. Lucius and I had a suspicion about who it might be."

"In trying to identify the bodies, the FBI checked the DNA of every one of them in the cistern plus Edgar's. Two of them are related," said Lucius. "It looks like Edgar is a direct paternal descendant about four or five generations removed—a distant grandson of number twenty-three, the one on the bottom. That last corpse has to be Henri Faustin! Bricks were mixed with his bones, so it looks like he was weighted down and thrown in. The pathologist confirmed no broken bones and the hyoid was intact, so he probably wasn't hanged or strangled. Also there were no cut marks or bullet fragments so that likely rules out stabbing and shooting. There's a good chance he was thrown in alive."

"Yuck!" exclaimed Genn. "Didn't that taint the water at the time?"

"Well, there appears to have been several inches of limey muck on the bottom and the forensic archaeologist thought the body sank into it and got partially covered over. The lack of oxygen and high pH slowed down decomposition, but gases would have bubbled up. It must have stunk pretty badly. But my guess is those left on the place ignored it until it went away. So, ol' Henri laid there for the next hundred years. Then after the big house burned, very little if any water flowed into the cistern and it eventually dried out. After all the bodies Edgar threw in got sorted out, Henri's bones had to be dug out by archaeologists the way those Indian burials were excavated at Moundville."

"There's more good news," said Lucius, "the detectives in Vestavia Hills and Atlanta got a couple of the suspects to talk. They got the ball rolling by cracking that surgeon from Vestavia Hills. He admitted paying to have his wife murdered by nitrogen asphyxiation and the disposal of her body. He never knew where they took her. The ones pulling off the murders are members of an underground gang known as the 'friends.' Edgar got to know some of them while at Parchman Farm."

"That's a strange name for a gang. I've never heard of them," said Dalton.

"'Friends' are a very different 'species.' They recruit better-educated members and don't use tattoos or signs to identify themselves. Plus they're very, very secretive and extremely loyal to the group. Cities don't even know they're around since they don't stake out 'turf' and avoid behavior that attracts attention. Their members can't wear dreads or weaves. They run drug and extortion rackets but only on the higher end. They never deal directly on the streets but only to distributors and professional athletes or celebrities. They also make big money carrying out hits for other gangs and wealthy individuals like Dunstan up in Vestavia Hills."

"Sherwyn that sounds like a book you need to write!" chimed in Dalton.

"But how did Edgar wind up in a group like that?" asked Genn.

"They recruited him as sort of a junior member or affiliate because he talked about his uncle's place and how isolated it is. Once he got out, they used it as a dumping ground for bodies. Gang members who didn't know Edgar would drive down to Big Tom and go in using the hidden key. They'd dump the bodies in the tall grass beside the road on the other side of the trees along that little branch. Each corpse had a plastic bag with a thousand dollars. They'd drop them off unannounced so there were no phone, text, or email messages that could be intercepted. If Edgar by chance ever encountered any gang members, he wouldn't tell them what he did with the bodies and apparently they didn't ask and didn't want to know. That way they couldn't rat him out and vice versa. Actually he only took the corpses a little ways up that road and dumped them into that old cistern. That was fine with the 'friends' since that lessened the amount of physical evidence that could be linked to them."

"So Edgar took in over twenty thousand dollars for just stuffing bodies down that hole," said Dalton.

"We found most of the money. Edgar hid it in a capped piece of PVC pipe buried behind the trailer. He put a handful of change in the bottom so a metal detector could locate it if he ever forgot the exact spot. We scanned the whole area lookin' for any metallic evidence and found it. Maybe he was planning to branch out on his own."

"I'm so glad this is getting resolved, but guys you know the best thing about all this?"

"What's that Genn?"

"That y'all didn't find two more bodies."

EPILOGUE

CONVERSATION AND LIGHT-HEARTED laughter filled the gallery at the Dinah Washington Cultural Arts Center in Tuscaloosa.

"Dr. Randolph, your show looks great and what a crowd for the reception!" said the gallery director.

A news reporter standing nearby added, "They're really enjoying your work and are intrigued by your dramatically lit landscapes. Those large format prints really pull the viewer into the scene."

Indeed many in the crowd gazed at the prints, but others gathered around a display case containing several objects—a bronzed pair of floppy old boots, a broken brick, and a sharpened metal strip partially wrapped in a dirty sock. Atop a small pedestal an old quarter with a carved death's head grinned at the viewers.

"Thanks for those kind words, but I think the image of the rainbow with the body in the shadows beyond the browse line is what attracted most of these people, especially after all the press coverage. People wanted to see the photo that started this saga and helped solve those murder cases."

"I can't blame them," said Genn in her green velvet

evening dress. "It was Dalton's eye that led to the solution of those murders and the breakup of a dangerous gang. But his bullheadedness almost got us killed!"

"Don't you look nice," said Genn as Billie Schroader and Sherwyn approached them.

"I have to admit that I don't wear girl clothes much, but look at me! I'm standing here with three Doctors of Philos-oh-phee!"

"Sherwyn, I've heard you and Billie are getting reacquainted," said Genn.

"Well, we've chatted quite a bit lately and I asked her to join us here tonight then we're going out to dinner later. I've never flown in a small plane before and she's invited me to come down to her place and she'll take me up."

"Sounds like fun," said Dalton. "It's about time you got your nose outta those moldy old papers and books."

"Billie promised me a good time. She's gonna make me a member of the 'Mile High Club,' whatever that is."

"Let's just say it'll be an uplifting experience," Dalton smirked. Genn ducked behind him quaking with suppressed laughter.

Billie arched her eyebrows and smiled beatifically.

ABOUT THE AUTHOR

JAMES N. (JIM) Ezell is a retired civil and environmental engineer. He is a native and lifelong resident of Alabama. A significant part of his youth was spent roaming the woods and fields of the Alabama Black Belt of Sumter County and the Piney Woods of Choctaw County in search of game, Indian artifacts, fossils, rocks, and adventure. As an undergraduate at the University of Alabama, he developed an appreciation and love of art, anthropology, history, music, and photography all of which remain as his avocations. In graduate school he pursued an engineering degree and worked as a consultant for a number of years. He also researched and wrote the text for the historical markers in Tuscaloosa's Government Plaza and Riverwalk. He currently writes a monthly column for Druid City Living and occasionally teaches in the University of Alabama's OLLI Program.

AUTHOR'S NOTE

TOMBIGBEE COUNTY EXISTS only in the imaginations of the author and readers. However, the name is that of a major river that begins in South Alabama as the west fork of the Mobile River. It extends for hundreds of river miles through West Alabama and crosses into East Mississippi near Columbus. The origin of the name Tombigbee has been the subject of speculation and legend for two centuries or more. "Bigbee" or "becbee" appears to derive from the Choctaw language and translates as "box-maker." One legend is based upon the prehistoric and early historic Choctaw custom of storing the bones of their dead in wooden boxes. It has been said that in the eighteenth century north of Mobile there lived a Spaniard named Tomás who built bone boxes for his friendly neighbors, the Chahta people or Choctaws. Thus the river that Tomás lived beside became known as the "Tombecbee" or as it is now called—the Tombigbee.

As previously stated the people and incidents portrayed in this novel are fictional. However, there is a cistern excavated by slaves into the chalk of the Alabama Black Belt on property belonging to relatives of the author. Decades ago a young man climbed through the narrow opening and descended into a dome shaped void that was so large a horse drawn wagon could be "driven around in a circle." At the bottom he discovered a corroded Winchester Model 1873 rifle. Near the site of the cistern, naturalized daffodils and iris bloom each spring and in the autumn the branches of an ancient Osage orange or "bodock" tree are laden with heavy green fruit.

Printed in the United States
By Bookmasters